CRAWLING
BETWEEN
EARTH
& HEAVEN

CRAWLING BETWEEN EARTH & HEAVEN

Sarah Beth Tarpenning

Glimfeather Press

Printed in the United States of America
ISBN: 978-1-971061-00-9

Published by Glimfeather Press
www.glimfeatherpress.com

Dedicated to Ray—my best friend

PROLOGUE

"Perception is reality. Objective truth is the enemy of progress."

— ELSINORE ANALYTICS INTERNAL MEMO, MARKETING COMPLIANCE v6.4

They said the fall lasted just under ten seconds. From the hundredth floor of Elsinore Analytics—his tower, his throne, his final lie—all the way down. Gravity didn't hesitate. Neither did the pavement.

They couldn't even open the casket.

Silas Eisler. CEO, husband, father … Dad.

They said he killed himself. That he'd overridden the divine fire-wall—a safeguard coded into every implant, freezing despair before it could reach muscle or nerve. Suicide had become impossible once they sanctified the firmware. No ledges, no belts, no exits. A liturgy in silicon, praying for the bereft. But Dad had written the code. He knew its backdoors, its cracks in the illusion. So it was believable he found a way through. The only question was, why?

Protesters clogged the plaza at the base of Elsinore Tower, bodies pressed shoulder to shoulder, the air damp with sweat and acrid drizzle. Their signs flickered with hand-painted ink or hacked neon rigs, jagged questions burning into the night:

"*Why him, not us?*"

"*Who codes mercy?*"

"*Autonomy now.*"

From his window, Harrow picked out a single sign near the barricades—cheap cardboard, the paint bleeding in the rain. A child's hand had written it, letters uneven: *Our father, not yours.* His throat tightened, but no sound came. He couldn't remember the last time he'd prayed, but if he had, it might've looked like that cardboard scrawl.

They weren't just shouting anymore, especially the veterans of the Substrate War. They were demanding answers. Why did the divine firewall lock them into life, while the programmer who wrote it had claimed a clean exit? The slogans rolled in waves, like data packets bouncing off stone.

"*Our bodies, our deaths.*"

"*We bled for your substrate.*"

"*Deliver us.*"

A month of this, every night, voices rising until they scraped the windows of the upper floors. A month of asking the same question and getting nothing but silence from the Tower.

Now Mom was moving on, into Uncle Viktor's bed. Into his arms. Into his shadow. A hostile takeover wrapped in silk sheets. The wedding invitations went out before the funeral flowers wilted.

Harrow stood by the window, watching the skyline ripple in the glass. Neon signs blinked in discordant rhythm, their colors bright and sickly—distractions to mask a system faking vitality. The air buzzed, electric and harsh. Elsinore stretched above and below, a vertical grave of mirrored steel and buried secrets. No windows opened. No walls breathed. It observed him like a god that never blinked.

Welcome to his own personal hell.

He turned away, his shoulders drooping as if gravity had become more oppressive overnight. His fingers brushed a small metal pendant at his collarbone—habit, not comfort—then dropped away. A tuxedo waited on the bed—clean, pressed, chrome-trimmed. Uniform, not attire. Elsinore's way of saying, "Play your part."

Fuck, he thought, scowling. *I've been cast as an extra.*

A soft chirp echoed in his skull. Neural ping—an incoming call to his AuRORA. The Augmented Reality Optical Relay Algorithm was a neural implant that monitored everything from bodily functions to communications. Everyone over the age of five had one.

Harrow tapped the sensor behind his ear. The interface flickered in his peripheral vision, a jarring flash of blue light against the dull gray of his room.

"Oh. My. God," Cassandra's voice burst out before he could answer.

"What?"

"My dad's losing it over forks and posture," she said. "Like if I nail the etiquette, it makes this circus less obscene. *Salad forks*, Harry. Not betrayal. Not bed-swapping. Salad forks."

Harrow snorted. "Show up, smile for the cameras, try not to

choke on the ashes."

"Right? Obvious shit. But no, he's like, 'Mind your posture, Cassandra, don't cross your legs during the toasts.' One more word and I'll strangle him with a linen napkin."

He smiled, but it didn't reach far. "He's only nervous. Rook could embarrass him. Again."

She laughed, low and sharp, like a flicked knife. It struck him somewhere beneath the ribs. "True. Last wedding we went to, he picked a fight before dessert."

"He was drunk."

"And *armed*."

Harrow chuckled. The dynamics of the Marr family always made for good stories.

A pause.

Harrow looked down at the tuxedo once more. It was still staring up at him.

"I gotta go," he said. "I haven't dressed yet."

There was silence on the other end. Then, softer: "Fuck, Harry. Missing the ceremony won't erase it."

"I know," he said. "God be with you."

"And with you."

He tapped the implant. Silence returned—sharp and familiar. He sat on the edge of the bed. The scent of ceremony lingered like incense clinging to clothes after Mass.

Then another chirp.

He groaned. Tapped the sensor again. "Smile and nod, hon. I gotta—"

But it wasn't Cassandra.

"Harr … Harr—ow … ow. Harr?"

The voice came in a glitch—fragments filled with static. It crawled through his AuRORA like rot in wiring. Garbled. A message chewed up and spat out by a dying machine.

Harrow froze.

The room narrowed. Cold light. White walls. Silent tux.

"Harr … ow. It's—"

He knew that voice.

Didn't matter how broken. Didn't matter how gone.

"Dad?" he said.

Silence—not absence, but rejection, a hiss crawling through the dead line.

CHAPTER 1

"The firewall blocks death. It does not block grief."

— Elsinore Analytics Internal Memo, Mental Health Subdivision

Friday, 22 June, 2136. It was a month after the wedding. The company planned a grand gala for Viktor, where music and dancing would fill the night.

Harrow stood near the edge of the ballroom, dressed head to toe in corporate mourning black. His suit was standard Elsinore issue for high-profile grief, perfectly tailored—but it felt like it belonged on someone else's skin. The fabric shimmered like oil on water: too smooth, too slick, too toxic. He kept his dagger—the mark of a gentleman—in a shoulder sheath. His face was set in stone—"please don't talk to me" etched into every line. It wasn't performative or dramatic. It was protective. A barrier between him and a world he no longer trusted.

He surveyed the room like a critic at a poor art show—looking for anything genuine and meaningful. Drones hovered overhead, trailing streams of colored light. Meanwhile, androids moved in perfect sync, delivering platters of molecular *hors d'oeuvres* around holographic centerpieces that flickered faintly if viewed from the wrong angle. Supposed to say "elegant." Instead, it looked like something created by an AI that mistook excess for tasteful.

Cassandra stood at the other end of the dance floor with her arms loosely crossed at her waist, poised yet relaxed. Her crimson cocktail dress highlighted the graceful lines of her figure, deliberately offset with the scuffed combat boots she wore underneath. Every few minutes, she looked toward Harrow and flashed a wry, knowing smile. He tried to avoid watching her, but he couldn't help himself. She attracted his attention like a static charge—light, invisible, yet inescapable. He would do anything to be alone with her.

He remembered a night on the maintenance deck, a week before the chaos—before death and betrayal. Cassandra had snuck a bottle of contraband synth-wine from Marr's reserves and lured him out under the pretext of "testing rooftop gravity fluctuation reports." They sat on a utility crate wrapped in thermal jackets, trading half-serious theories about the stars beyond the dome. She claimed some were fakes—repurposed satellites mimicking constellations. He'd laughed. She'd said, "Not paranoid. Just paying attention." He recalled how she touched his cheek then—quick, unceremonious. Like flipping a switch.

Cassandra's brother, Rook, approached Harrow and nodded a greeting, bringing him back to the present. Rook shifted his weight—subtle, yet not casual. The set of his jaw and the way his eyes kept drifting to the far wall all conveyed a sense of distance.

He was present, physically, in the aftermath of death. But the rest of him was already somewhere else. Neo-Paris, perhaps. Rooftop bars, backroom meetings, places where people talked fast and trusted slowly. He wore his jacket unzipped, slightly off code. His dagger lay in an open sheath at his waist. A deliberate statement.

"Some scene, huh?" he said.

Harrow shrugged.

The air smelled fake—an algorithm's version of freshness, too pristine to be natural. It stuck in Harrow's throat. Somewhere far below, muffled by the tower's triple-pane glass, came the rhythmic pulse of protest chants. Too faint for the guests to take notice, too persistent for him to forget. Outside, the streets seethed; inside, the marble gleamed.

"Dad is annoying as ever," Rook continued. "Argued with Cassandra for over an hour about those fucking boots."

"I like those fucking boots," Harrow said.

Rook chuckled.

Harrow glanced at the table where his mother and Viktor would sit. Sure enough, Director Marr was finishing up the last decorations before the start of the gala. Holo-ads displayed dopamine teas, comfortware, and synthetic intimacy—luxuries for people too wealthy to feel bad. The colors moved in a slow, predatory dance, casting flickering reflections on the floor. Life had been like this since the end of the Substrate War, when Elsinore secured the substrate needed for AuRORA.

The guests were already mingling.

Harrow stood at the edge of everything, hands in his pockets, taking in the noise. All of it—the polished drones, the synthetic air, the silent grief of a son forced to smile for investors.

He shrugged. "Your dad just wants everything to be perfect for …"

Rook raised his cybernetic arm and put its hand on Harrow's shoulder. "I know, man," he said. "I know."

The doors opened with a smooth hydraulic hiss. A synthesized fanfare followed—precise and coded. Celebration lacking soul.

Viktor entered first.

The new CEO, Harrow's uncle. His silhouette alone spoke volumes—upright, centered, poised. The exosuit he wore was custom-made, trimmed in polished nanosteel and brushed polymer, designed to project power without relying on brute force. Only men as wealthy as Viktor could afford the luxury of such protection. AuRORAs gleamed at his temples, pulsing iris-blue with the smug precision of a man who'd updated both firmware and faith in the same afternoon. His gaze swept across the room—a predator's calm evaluation—each detail registering with unnerving accuracy. Not unkind, merely efficient.

At his side, his wife and CFO, Corra, moved with deliberate grace. Her dress was dark and subtle, shaped to suggest presence without drawing attention. Her shoes made no sound on the marble—silence that was bought and polished. She didn't look at Harrow, nor did she need to; her awareness of him was complete: a mother's instinct, hidden behind walls of propriety and performance.

Viktor stepped onto the dance floor with a look of confidence he had developed with hours in front of the mirror. He said the right things: grief, duty, the burden of the crown settling on his brow. Mourner and monarch in one act, transforming tragedy into a quarterly pivot. A necessary duty in the corporate timeline. Mourn, yes, but don't let mourning slow down progress. "God," he said, "would want us to move on now."

He called it a sad joy, a bittersweet unity, marrying Harrow's mother in the wake of his father's death. He said everyone had advised him to marry Corra, as though it were part of an onboarding process. It was an honor, he said, to take up Silas' mantle and run Elsinore Analytics.

The board applauded, of course. None of them were about to call out the new CEO for "complex emotional optics."

Viktor turned to Rook. The change was subtle—a tilt of the head and a narrowing of the eyes. Impatience masqueraded as interest. "I hear *you* put in for a transfer."

Rook met his gaze. "I want Neo-Paris. I know the city. I can make it work."

Viktor examined Rook's cybernetic arm, an injury he sustained while working as a security guard. It was more than just hardware; it represented history. Four years earlier, a protest outside Elsinore Tower turned chaotic. He was armed with little more than a badge and a half-spent stun baton. The crowd surged forward, fire in their hands, and Silas Eisler was caught in the chaos. Rook threw himself between the CEO and the mob, taking the brunt of the attack. The firebomb that shredded his arm should have ended his career. Instead, it shaped him. Surgeons rebuilt the limb with alloy and nerve-mesh, and when he went back to work, he carried himself with the same steady resolve.

Even Viktor had marked it at the time—how courage could forge a leader, how fire could temper loyalty. Rook hadn't just protected Silas; he'd demonstrated that he was a man willing to stand against the line of flames.

"What does your father say?" Viktor asked. "He is your boss, after all."

Marr exhaled softly, not with disapproval but with resignation. Ambition without permission is inefficient.

Viktor nodded once. "Go. Neo-Paris is your concern now. I'll appoint you head of security at Versailles Tower."

Quick. Clean. Unnoticed. Like everything else in this building, the exchange was designed for function, not for feeling.

Viktor turned to Harrow. "My nephew," he said, then, too heavily, "my son."

His voice sounded sincere, yet it lacked the resonance of genuine feeling. No affection—only protocol.

Harrow didn't respond, staying still and unreadable. He was the calm, unmoving core of a room built to keep moving.

Viktor stepped closer. "Why are you being so difficult?"

"I'm not your son," Harrow said.

Viktor didn't blink.

Corra stepped forward, her eyes searching Harrow's face. "Harry, please," she said with gentle intensity. "Viktor has a surprise for you."

"Yes," Viktor said. "Yes. I know you intend to complete your graduate work this year. But with your father gone, I think it's time for you to take your rightful place in the executive suite. You are an *heir* after all."

Harrow raised an eyebrow.

"It will give you an opportunity to try out the reins," Cora said. "And it will help take your mind off things."

"Things?" Harrow stepped back. "You mean Dad."

"Grief needs structure," Viktor said. "And Elsinore needs you presentable."

Harrow frowned.

"I'm making you Executive Vice President over Corporate Security," Victor said. "You will coordinate interdepartmental security protocols. If you find any issues, report directly to me. If you like, you can bring Cassandra up to work with you."

"Please take the position," Corra said. "For me?"

Harrow sighed. "Fine. For you."

It sounded like surrender. But there was no surrender in him—only mere quiet submission.

Viktor faced the crowd and raised his glass.

"To unity."

The room reverberated with the clink of glassware. Harrow didn't raise his.

He bowed his head to his mother, a silent goodbye, then walked out into the quiet hallway.

Once alone, the ballroom doors closed behind him, Harrow threw his glass against the wall. Let out a scream. Pressed his hands to a cold steel table. "*Libera me*," he muttered—deliver me—under his breath. Not to be heard even by himself.

God, if only he could dismantle this physical form, this flawed code of existence. Melt it away. Erase the corrupted program. Leave only vapor on the mirror.

But the divine firewall still forbade suicide—his father's firewall. A hard-coded prohibition, stitched into every neural implant by the man who believed death should never be an option. He meant it as mercy, or maybe as control. Either way, it persisted. You can't jump, can't slice, can't even walk into traffic without the system intercepting your intent. Locked out of the only clean exit by a rulebook that no one reads but everyone fears—like the catechism you stopped believing but never stopped reciting. And the irony? His father was the first to bypass it.

And so, Harrow woke up again. Every day. Dragging this husk through more boardroom theater while the world rotted from the inside. Everything felt flatlined. Stale. Like old coffee and yesterday's data.

Two months. Not even that long. His father, barely cooled in the grave. The vultures had already nested on his throne.

His father had been regal and righteous. The air crackled around him; he embodied Olympus.

Viktor? Roadside trash with a crown pulled from the burn bin.

And Corra. *God.* His father looked at her with the same reverence someone might have for an angel visiting a grand cathedral. She clung to him as if gravity had shifted just for them.

Now?

Only a month out, and she had rebooted, laughing beside the man who sank into his father's absence like a virus.

She wore the same shoes for the wedding as she had worn to

the funeral.

This wasn't grief. It was betrayal wearing a designer dress.

He couldn't express what he truly felt. Couldn't shout the truth into a room full of liars.

So he carried it.

Until I break.

And I will.

Heavy boots thudded against synthetic flooring.

Harrow's best friend, Pax, was the first to approach. A security guard named Bjørn followed closely behind. Both of them looked tense, eyes sharp with unspoken concern.

"Hey, Harry," Pax said cautiously. "Or should I say *Mr. Executive VP?*"

Harrow thought of another night—the two of them outside a dive in the Neon, Harrow bleeding from a fight he shouldn't have picked. Pax had dragged him into the rain, slammed him against a wall, and said, "You want to fall apart, fine—but not where they can watch." Then Pax had stood with him until the tremors stopped. Harrow remembered the water running down his face, rain or tears, he couldn't tell. And Pax saying nothing more, just existing between Harrow and collapse.

Harrow turned, a flicker of relief washed over him. He gripped Pax's hand tightly.

"Pax," he said. "A rare line of clean code in a corrupted system. Bjørn. What's up?"

"We have news," Pax said. "About your father."

Harrow sat at the table. "My father—God, I swear I just saw

him."

Pax sat down next to him. "Where, Harry?"

"In my head. A flicker. A ghost in the feed."

"I knew him well," Pax said. "Back before everything cracked. A towering figure. Ran Elsinore like it was in his blood."

"Dad was awesome," Harrow said.

Pax hesitated, leaned forward. "I think I saw him again last night."

Harrow furrowed his brows. "Who?"

"Your father."

"What are you saying?"

"Just hold on," Pax said, leaning closer. "Let me lay it out—Bjørn was on the night rotation, patrolling the high catwalks. Two nights in a row, just past 0300, he clocked a figure on the thermal cams. Looked exactly like your father—same stride, same exosuit, high-grade, full-spec. Walked past him, calm, precise, like he was still running the company. Bjørn froze. Couldn't speak. Just watched it drift past like time itself skipped a beat. Third night, I joined Bjørn. Swore I'd see for myself. And I did. Same silhouette. Same movements. I knew your father, Harrow. That thing out there … it could've been him, down to the last microgesture."

Harrow considered this a moment before asking: "Where did this happen?"

Bjørn responded: "On the rooftop platform where I'm posted. Northeast quadrant."

"You tried interfacing with it?"

"Yeah," Pax said, "I spoke. Got nothing back. But—once—it

lifted its head, like it was syncing with me. Then the curfew siren kicked in. Loud. Jarring. And it glitched. Twitched. Then it was just gone. Like it was never there."

Harrow frowned. "That's… unnerving."

"I'd stake my neural feed on it," Pax said. "We debated reporting it up the chain, but figured it should go straight to you and let you *coordinate*."

"You were right," Harrow said. "I don't like the feel of this. Are you posted again tonight?"

"Yes, sir," Bjørn said. "Same slot."

"You said it was armed?" Harrow asked.

"Fully equipped, sir," Bjørn said.

"Head to toe?"

"Full combat frame," Bjørn said. "Looked regulation-grade."

"Then the face was concealed?" Harrow asked.

"No—visor was up. Face was visible," Pax said.

"Did he seem hostile?"

"No," Pax said. "Not rage. Grief. Like … like something had been lost he couldn't reclaim."

"Coloration? Skin tone?"

"Drained. No flush," Pax said. "Ghost-white."

"Did he make eye contact?"

Pax took a deep breath and let it out slowly. "Locked eyes the whole time. Never looked away."

"I wish I'd seen it," Harrow said.

"You'd have been stunned."

"No doubt," Harrow said. "How long did it stay visible?"

"Long enough to count a clean hundred. Maybe less."

Bjørn shook his head. "Felt longer."

"Not when I was there," Pax said.

"Beard still streaked with silver?" Harrow asked.

Pax nodded. "Exactly how I remember it. Dark brown, silver tracing through. Just like before."

Harrow remained silent for a full minute as he thought about the implications of what Pax and Bjørn had told him. Finally, he said: "Then I'm coming tonight. If that thing shows up again, I'll confront it myself. Even if the entire grid yells at me to stand down. Listen—if you've kept this off comms so far, keep it that way. Total blackout. No chatter. Think about what you've seen, but don't talk about it to anyone. I'll meet you on the platform between 2300 and midnight."

"We'll be there," Bjørn said. "Standing by."

"More than duty—what I need is loyalty. Friendship. You have mine."

"And ours in return," said Pax.

Harrow touched two fingers briefly to his temple before saying, "God be with you."

"And with you," Pax said.

Pax and Bjørn left Harrow.

My father's specter, armored, Harrow thought, *patrolling old ground. This reeks. Something's wrong in the system—I can feel it. I need night to fall. Corrupt code doesn't stay buried forever; it always surfaces.*

The door to the ballroom slid open with a sigh, and Cassandra peeked out, her hair tucked behind one ear, her lips curling into a sly yet gentle smile. When she saw Harrow standing alone in the hallway, her smile grew wider.

That smile—God, he remembered the first time he saw it. Back then, no ballrooms, no algorithms measuring the angle of her gaze. Just a rusted rooftop in the Neon, wind cutting cold across the skyline. He'd been railing against the world, drunk on cheap synth, ready to smash something just to feel alive. She'd laughed—light, startling—and taken the bottle from his hand. "If you break everything, Harry, there'll be nothing left for us to dance on." Then she'd pulled him into a clumsy sway, no music but the hum of traffic below, her forehead pressed to his. It had been enough to silence him. Enough to make him want more.

"Come dance with me," Cassandra said.

Harrow shifted his weight. "I dunno."

"Come on." She leaned her shoulder against the frame, casual, but her eyes made it clear this wasn't optional. "Your mom is worried, and Viktor doesn't like how this looks."

He rolled his eyes. "That makes me want to go in less."

She brightened.

"One dance," he said firmly.

"Three."

"Two."

"Deal."

With a grin to mark this small victory over the chaos, she pulled the door wider. Music spilled out—bass-heavy, overly polished, curated by some Elsinore algorithm substituting rhythm for joy. Harrow followed her inside.

The gala lights stung—soft gold over white marble, designed to mimic warmth but without actual heat. People spun beneath the chandeliers in designer armor, smiling as if compliance were a performance grade.

Before he could change his mind, Cassandra turned and caught him by the shoulders.

"No backing out," she said.

She slid one hand behind his neck, the other at his side. He set his palms at her waist, trying to look like a man who belonged in his own skin. She leaned in—closer than polite, unapologetic. They moved—not perfectly, not smoothly—but enough to satisfy the onlookers and the feed. Overhead, a drone adjusted its orbit; the music brightened by half a decibel, like the room itself was trying to smile.

Her breath brushed his jaw. "There. Not so hard."

"It is when everyone's watching."

"They always are," she said. "Might as well give them a good frame."

Her combat boot nudged his instep—a faint tap in time no one else would notice. He felt something slide into his palm—thin, cold, laminated. An access card.

"Hold that," she murmured, lips barely moving. "Rooftop access. You didn't get it from me."

"How did you—"

She touched a finger to his mouth. The *shh* was soft, but the look wasn't. Then, with her voice pitched just louder—performance level—she added, "Terrible playlist. If I hear one more faux-jazz loop I'm filing a complaint."

He let a laugh out for the cameras. She used it to cover the whisper against his cheek: "Northeast service stair. Badge pings green only once. Cams stutter at fifty-nine on the hour—thirty seconds of snow. If anyone asks what we were talking about, it was the playlist."

"Cassandra—"

"Don't look at the walls," she said, still smiling. "Marr reads lips. Keep yours moving."

He swallowed, and the card vanished into his cuff like it had always been there. The chant from the street bled through the marble—three muffled beats, then silence—just enough to remind him what waited outside the glass.

"Head up," she said, guiding him through a turn. "Pretend you're capable of joy."

"I'm not."

"Then borrow mine," she said, and for half a breath he believed her.

They drifted to a stop at the edge of the floor. She kept her smile on for the room and pressed the smallest warning into his palm with her fingertips. He touched his forehead to hers and exhaled.

CHAPTER 2

"Authority should be expressed as advice. Ownership is best internalized."

— ELSINORE ANALYTICS FAMILY INTEGRATION MANUAL, SECTION 3.7

Hours later, Cassandra and Rook stood next to an Auto-Cab, a self-driving transport that hovered above the ground. Its hum pulsed with smug certainty—the confidence of a machine that had never been late and expected to outlive everyone around it. The doors hung open, wide and toothless: a corporate deity offering safe passage, for now.

"You don't have to go," Cassandra said.

Rook smiled.

He adjusted the straps of his carryall—not because anything was loose; Rook didn't do loose—but because the ritual grounded him. It was a soldier's tic from training, paired with a quick touch to the medallion beneath his shirt. He wasn't running; only redeploying. Neo-Paris called: ultratech, illicit deals, and nihilistic charm.

It didn't ask questions—just scanned your ID and handed you a drink or a gun, depending on the district.

"The data uplink's fast," he said. "No excuses. Keep in touch."

She stood with her arms crossed, adopting a pose that was both protective and defiant. Her jacket was temperature-controlled; the cold stemmed from within. She watched him like a bird flying toward a window: oblivious and destined to strike.

Her eyes glinted with affection but also with disappointment. She wasn't sure if her feelings of discontent came from his desire to disappear in Neo-Paris or because he was leaving her behind. No matter, Rook—as always—would impulsively charge forward and likely end up bleeding before he knew he was cut.

A chemical breeze brushed past them, infused with engineered florals and synthetic ozone—Elsinore's version of fresh air. It clung to the back of the throat.

Behind them, the city pulsed. Neon bled through the clouds filled with corrupted dreams: perfume, propaganda, funeral insurance. At street level, knots of protesters clogged the avenues, their chants dampened to a wet hiss by engineered rain. Cassandra had weaved her way through them to get from her flat to the tower, the spray cold on her skin, and for a moment she considered joining the throng. She glanced up—not searching—just letting the overhead lens know she'd thought about it.

Now, Cassandra stood with Rook in the quiet buffer between the tower and the edge of the world.

"Listen," he said. "About Harrow—don't take him at face value."

Cassandra arched an eyebrow. "Oh?"

He gazed out over the city. Words felt easier out there. "He's performing. They all are. Every heir. Every legacy. You don't get to feel things when you're the heir of the corporate gods."

Her expression cooled.

"What do you mean?"

He turned back slowly. "Even if it's real—it won't matter. Elsinore has already written his destiny. The board doesn't care who he loves. They care who he marries. And whether his bride will be an asset."

She didn't blink.

Then she smiled.

"That's a shame," she said, pulling her hair back into a ponytail.

"I'm not saying he doesn't care," Rook said. "But if you fall too deep—no matter what he feels, in the end, he won't choose you."

He didn't look at her. Just out, across the Neon, toward the distant towers slicing the sky.

"I don't want to find you alone in some flat," he said, "drinking what's left in the bottle, replaying songs that weren't about you, trying to figure out what you did wrong."

Cassandra looked down. Neon danced in oil-slick puddles. Mocking colors.

"Do you remember?" Rook asked. "Remember life in the Neon?"

She nodded. Life in the Neon had been all rust and rot, the air thick with engine grease and the sickly sweet perfume of decay. They'd lived four to a room in a housing stack with flickering power and fungus on the walls, where her mother coughed herself hollow while Marr hustled from job to job—mechanic one week, informant the next. He wasn't "Director Marr" then. Just a man with sharp eyes and iron will, working his way up by selling some secrets and keeping others. Cassandra remembered the stench of melting plastic, the neon ads that bled through the cracked windows, and the way kids disappeared during curfew, and no one asked why. She had learned to be quiet there. To watch. To archive. Survival didn't mean fighting—it meant mastering social camouflage.

"Because," Rook continued, "men like Harrow don't marry girls from the Neon. You had best remember that."

"I'll remember," Cassandra said. Clipped. Controlled.

She leaned in and kissed his cheek.

"You sound like someone who's seen too much and call disillusionment wisdom," she said.

He didn't move.

"You keep warning me about the fall," she said. "Maybe I don't mind the fall. It's the landing that breaks you after all."

"Maybe," Rook said.

The Auto-Cab waited.

"Rook!"

Their father.

His voice sliced through the air like a blade. His coat billowed behind him. His augmented eyes flickered with scrolling data—private channels, live feeds, encrypted intent.

"One minute," Marr said, already mid-scroll. "Board briefing changed again. Twice."

He reached them, his hand resting on Rook's shoulder like a mark of ownership.

"Go," he said. Then, quieter: "But listen."

Rook remained silent. Cassandra rolled her eyes.

Marr ignored them both.

"Don't say everything you think. Don't act on impulse. Trust slow. Speak less. Own less. Don't flaunt wealth. And above all—"

The Auto-Cab pinged. Time's up.

He raised a finger.

"—be true to yourself."

A pause. Rook inclined his head in a nod that resembled the one given after a prayer.

Cassandra clapped Rook gently on the shoulder. "You heard him."

Rook almost smiled. Almost.

"I hear you, Father."

He turned to Cassandra. His voice softened. "God be with you."

"And with you," she said. Plain. Clean. A door, gently shut.

He hesitated.

"Don't forget what I told you."

"I won't."

Then he stepped into the transport. The doors sealed with a sigh, and the cab rose then vanished.

Silence.

Director Marr exhaled. Not emotion. Procedure. He turned to Cassandra.

"What did he say?"

She hesitated. The truth was too fragile.

"Something about Harrow."

Marr didn't react, but his lenses twitched.

"Ah." A trigger, not a reply.

His tone cooled. Calculated.

"How long have you two been together?"

Her jaw clenched. He knew; he was baiting her.

Cassandra and Harrow had been together four years—long enough to burn through the infatuation, long enough to see each other at their worst, and still come back. They met in the cracks between their worlds: he was the son of Elsinore's founder, she was the girl who'd clawed her way out of the Neon. On paper, they had nothing in common. In practice, they recognized each other instantly—two people who didn't quite belong where they'd been born.

What held them was as much survival as affection. She knew when to pull him back from the edge, when his anger threatened to burn him down. He knew when to respect her silence, when words would only reopen old wounds. They built small rituals out of the chaos: late nights on rooftops, trading secrets, mapping the city lights like constellations only they understood.

They loved each other with a kind of defiance. Against family, against Elsinore, against the inevitability of collapse. Beneath it all, the cracks were there. Cassandra wondered if he carried his father's darkness. Harrow wondered if she stayed with him for love, or for leverage against the Tower. Neither of them asked.

What they had was fragile. What they had was unbreakable.

Four years proved both could be true.

"And has he told you he loves you?"

A pause. "Yes."

He scoffed. No warmth. Merely strategy.

"Do you believe him?"

She could have lied. She didn't. "I don't know."

He scanned her—his eyes flickering, absorbing more than only her words.

"Then let me tell you what to think."

He stepped closer. Lights illuminated his face in chrome and blue.

"You're young. Naive. He's not a man. He's a symbol. A stock option in waiting. And you—"

She stared at him.

"Do you realize what it's taken to get us here?"

Cassandra frowned. Her father fought in the Substrate War— soldier, spy, survivor. Rook was a baby then; Cassandra came after. They lived in the Neon, Marr scraping to provide, powerless as his wife fell ill. Things only turned when Elsinore hired him for security.

"Do you value yourself so little?" he asked.

Cassandra didn't move.

"Don't make a fool of me," he said, quiet and sharp.

She swallowed. "I love him."

Marr laughed—dry, cruel.

"Oh, I'm sure you do. That's the trick. Make the mark feel chosen. Make them hand it all over."

She said nothing. Her silence was its own defiance.

He adjusted his collar.

"You'll be more careful," he said. "No more private meetings. That's final."

She stared past him, to the glitching skyline. In her pocket, her thumb rubbed the smooth face of an old coin with Saint Expeditus' image worn flat.

"I will obey, Father," she said.

The tone was soft. The meaning wasn't.

She turned and walked away. Heels steady. Shoulders squared.

Cassandra threaded her way through the crowd, shoulder to shoulder with strangers whose faces burned with anger and lost hope. Their chants rose and fell like the tide, echoing against the glass towers until it seemed as though the whole city was shouting. Cardboard signs slapped in the wind, neon paint still wet, slogans dripping defiance. For a moment, she wanted to stop—wanted to raise her voice, throw her fury into theirs, let the noise burn her throat raw. But she kept moving. Somewhere above, hidden optics swept the streets, and she knew one careless second would be enough for her father to tag her in a feed. Marr's eyes were everywhere. So, she pushed forward, jaw tight, each step a silent promise. If she couldn't scream here in the open, she'd find other ways. The real protest would have to live in shadows.

The protests had a complicated history, all of it rooted in the Substrate War.

Twenty-five years back, the world bled for substrate. Rare, volatile, worth more than water. Not just fuel—identity. Without it, implants glitched, memory-sync shredded, AI cores went dumb, whole districts blinked out like dead pixels. Families bartered food rations for maintenance cycles, deciding who got to keep their mind intact, who went dark.

Wars weren't fought for land anymore. They were fought for veins of powdered thought. Nations dropped armies, corps dropped contractors, syndicates dropped bodies in the street. Districts turned feral when the lines snapped. Soldiers didn't just lose battles—they lost themselves. A week without substrate and your head filled with static until you weren't you anymore.

Silas Eisler was an engineer then, young and already dangerous with code. He was supposed to be writing stability protocols. Instead, he watched humanity short-circuit in real time—executives slumping mid-pitch, grunts twitching in the mud, civilians keeling over on subway floors. Suicide surged. Nobody wanted to stay unplugged, trapped in a body that no longer felt like theirs.

Then came the chem strike. Neon district, east side. A hundred thousand cut off overnight. Ten thousand brains melted in the first week. Suicide spread like contagion—if one went, others followed, in a morbid chain reaction. Parents dragged kids with them. Lovers synced exits in perfect timing. Whole families dived together because one fracture was enough to break the rest. Death wasn't private anymore—it was viral.

That's what Silas saw. Not choice. Not despair. A system crash running skull to skull. And so he wrote the patch. Hard-coded prohibition. No self-termination. No clean exit. No final say. He called it the divine firewall. Marketed it as mercy: *"No one will ever be forced to watch their family vanish again."* But everyone knew the other side. Autonomy stripped. Grief weaponized. Corporations inheriting ownership of your body with the flick of a switch.

History calls it the Substrate War. The streets call it the Suicide Wars. The firewall stopped the bleed, but it also locked every skull to the system. Silas walked out of it a prophet-engineer, savior of humanity. But the whispers never stopped: he didn't save anyone. He just locked the world inside a cage.

There had been protests before—angry clusters at tower gates, marches through the Neon—but Cassandra had never seen anything on this scale. The streets seethed with it, chants hammering the glass facades like waves against stone. And all of it circling the same bitter irony: how could Silas Eisler hard-code a law into every skull but his own? He built the cage and kept the key. Cassandra felt it too, a slow boil in her veins. She didn't want to die, but the fact that she had no right to choose gnawed at her. Every breath was a lease. Every heartbeat rented. That truth—no matter how polished the corporate spin—made her want to scream until her throat tore.

She reached the mid-residential stack and looked back at the crowd gathered under Elsinore Tower. "Burn it down," she muttered, and keyed the door.

CHAPTER 3

"All systems must submit to audit. Even legacy."

— DATA PURITY DOCTRINE, LINE 108

Harrow shoved his hands further into his pockets. His father's voice, long buried, surfaced as distorted static—not a memory, but noise. Elsinore hadn't just buried Silas Eisler; it had rebranded him.

But once, the voice hadn't been static. Once it had filled every room. Harrow remembered standing beside him on the mezzanine floor of Elsinore, watching the employees file out after a quarterly announcement. Silas had leaned close, his words low enough that only Harrow could hear: "Power isn't volume, Harry. It's resonance. Speak once and make it echo." The crowd below had dispersed in orderly silence, every mind already turning his words into law. Harrow had believed then that nothing could fracture that kind of presence. That his father was welded into the bones of the tower itself.

Harrow and Pax trudged toward the rooftop security platform, collars up, shoulders hunched, silence heavy between them. The cold here didn't bite — it burrowed. Through coats. Through skin. The wind howled through the concrete arteries of Elsinore Analytics, shrill and restless, like a bored god experimenting with sound. Somewhere above, a loose panel rattled as if revealing an uneasy truth.

A gust slipped beneath Harrow's jacket, fingers of frost curled along his spine with practiced malice. He flinched, muttered something under his breath, and kept walking.

Pax endured the cold just as he did everything else—with stoic patience and the demeanor of someone who knew life without comfort. He surveyed the hazy horizon, wary of what it might reveal. Harrow trusted him more than anyone, a trust that grew exponentially as the number of people Harrow had left dwindled.

Pax broke the silence. "You don't have to go through with this."

Harrow said nothing, lips moving in a fragment of an old prayer he no longer believed in, but couldn't quite stop reciting.

The skyline loomed—a fever dream of neon and concrete. Glitching billboards screamed half-truths. Buildings flickered. One pulsed a binary warning across its glass facade: *YOU ARE BEING WATCHED*. Far below, protesters clustered in the avenues, their banners were shards of color in the monochrome sprawl. From this height, their chants bled into the wind—more vibration than voice—but the rhythm was unmistakable: steady, stubborn, impossible to ignore.

Bjørn waited at the rooftop edge, arms crossed tightly, jaw clenched against the wind. His shoulders slumped, a look of regret on his face, as he seemed to be contemplating his life choices.

Harrow adjusted the thermal settings of his coat. The response was sluggish and lukewarm. It served as a reminder that, despite all the technology humanity had created—conscious algorithms, cloned memories, synthetic immortality—no one had made a jacket that actually worked.

Pax exhaled. "Cold as regret," he said.

"What time is it?" Harrow asked, squinting at the bruised sky.

Pax nodded at the glitching clock tower. Its hands twitched as if they were stuck buffering.

"Not quite midnight."

Bjørn didn't look up. "It struck."

He'd checked. Twice.

Then the wind fell still.

And everything started to feel wrong.

A burst of blinding light exploded from the corporate district— bright and sudden. The sky flashed, gold and lavender spilling over the clouds. From deep within Elsinore, bass-heavy music pulsed upward. Synthetic horns followed.

Pax squinted. "What the fuck is that?"

Harrow didn't blink. "Viktor. Celebrating." He let the word curdle in his mouth. "Quarterly projections. Mergers. Toasts to ghosts."

"It's a tradition?" Pax asked.

"Sure. Like ritual sacrifice. But with better lighting."

The skyline shimmered. Harrow remembered being a boy on the observation deck, his father's hand heavy on his shoulder. *Every system rots if you let it,* Silas had said, voice like iron. *Not because it's corrupt, but because people forget what it cost to build.*

Now, Viktor's fireworks mocked that memory—neon confetti scattered across a grave.

Pax nudged him. "You talk like the empire's already dead."

"It is. Survivors inherit the legacy. Doesn't matter who built it." Harrow exhaled, eyes fixed on the chaos below. "All it takes is one fracture. One person to rise up. One voice to echo."

Bjørn twitched. "Look."

A figure flickered at the rooftop's edge.

Not walking. Not approaching. Just … existing. One frame at a time.

It glitched into being.

The shape wavered—jagged edges, light distorted. A form too unstable to render. Harrow felt it in his teeth. In his spine. The hum of a presence that was wrong in ways language couldn't convey.

Human. But not. Or no longer.

It twitched between forms. Old ceremonial dress. Black armor. Nothing at all. A memory in rewind.

Harrow stiffened. A tremor passed through his breath. He crushed it.

Not fear.

Curiosity like a blade behind his ribs.

His heart rate spiked. His neural HUD blinked amber: *BIO-METRICS UNSTABLE.*

He didn't care.

He stepped forward.

"Angels," he said. "And ministers of grace… defend us."

The ghost said nothing.

It watched.

And Harrow knew it was there for him.

The figure flickered. One moment a man, the next a rupture — code tearing at the seams. Light shimmered from within. Reality blinked.

Its face kept shifting. Expressions from Harrow's childhood— and expressions that never belonged to his father at all. The mouth opened. The sound arrived late.

A time-glitch. A memory fracture.

Harrow forced breath into his lungs.

"Are you a benevolent spirit," he asked, steady but brittle, "or something clawed out of the digital abyss?"

No response.

"A corrupted backup? A wraith of code and shattered files? Or a ghost?"

His throat closed.

"Then I'll name you." He drew a slow breath. "Silas Eisler. Father."

The ghost twitched.

It raised an arm—slow, jerky, puppet-like. The motion defied grace.

Then it pointed. Directly at Harrow.

The world held its breath.

And then it beckoned.

Not an invitation.

A summons.

Bjørn stepped back. Not out of fear. Out of instinct.

"It's calling you," he said. The words made him flinch.

Pax reached out, hand hovering near Harrow's sleeve. "Don't follow it. You don't know what it is—or what's underneath."

Harrow didn't blink. "It won't speak. But it doesn't have to."

He stepped forward.

Pax grabbed him. "You don't come back from some paths. You don't know where it ends."

Harrow turned. Calm, cold.

"I have nothing to lose."

The ghost beckoned again.

Bjørn moved to block him. "We don't know what it is."

"Move," Harrow said. Flat. Inevitability incarnate.

Pax tried once more. "What if it breaks you? What if you're not you anymore?"

Harrow met his gaze. A flicker of grief.

"It calls to me," he said. "And I will follow."

And he did.

Before either of them could stop him.

He stepped into the glitching cold.

The ghost turned.

They vanished.

Only silence remained.

And Elsinore exhaled.

Harrow stalked the rooftop corridors, each step sharper than the last, with boots echoing off damp concrete in a rhythm that felt like a countdown. A thick, metallic smell of rust and damp stone lingered heavily in the air, blending with the musty odor of long-forgotten secrets. This was decay by design—rot preserved in corporate amber.

His nerves screamed. Not adrenaline—something colder. A wrongness in the air, quiet but persistent. A system error ready to surface.

The overhead lights buzzed and flickered in shades of sickly pink and corporate white. They blinked like dying stars—too dim to be helpful and too persistent to ignore. Somewhere deep in his skull, a sarcastic voice whispered: Don't be the guy in the horror movie who follows the ghost.

But he kept going.

He hated that he wanted to run. Hated more that he couldn't.

His cybernetic eyes futilely tried to track the figure ahead. Top-tier hardware, and still it jittered in and out of focus, as if the ghost didn't exist in any single frame. Humanoid. Then not. His father. Then something wearing him like code.

Error messages flared in his vision: INCOMPLETE RENDER. UNKNOWN PROTOCOL. DO NOT FOLLOW.

He followed.

The air grew heavy. Static clung to his skin, a creepy, buzzing feeling that seemed alive and prickly. Breathing became difficult. Each inhale tasted metallic.

The corridor narrowed. Too tight. The building was herding him forward. Harrow flexed his hands, shaking off the tremor from his fingers. He told himself it was interference. Told himself it was nonsense.

He was lying.

The ghost stopped.

So did Harrow.

Inhale. Hold. Exhale. Repeat. It was the only rhythm he trusted.

"Where are you leading me?" he asked, forcing calm.

The ghost turned.

Its face struggled to form. Jagged pixels strained to create a corrupted likeness. Glowing eyes. Lips that moved out of sync. No expression. No warmth. A lagging simulation.

"Listen," it said.

The word cut.

Harrow flinched inward.

His father's voice. But hollow. Stripped of everything human.

"I will," Harrow said. The words felt foreign.

The ghost flickered intensely, with edges breaking into flickering streaks of light. Cracks spiderwebbed across its form like shattered glass.

"The time is near. I must return to the system."

The ghost pulsed with static, a broadcast degrading by the second. Its signal unraveling.

"The firewalls will soon consume what remains."

Something clenched in Harrow's chest. It wasn't fear but a quiet, helpless fury. A frustrated, simmering rage builds when you lash out blindly, unable to strike at the source of your torment.

"Poor ghost," he said.

"Do not pity me," it said.

The voice struck sharp now, static-laced and dangerous.

"Listen."

Harrow braced.

"If you ever loved me—"

The words detonated inside him.

His hands curled into fists, nails carving crescents into his palms.

"Oh, God," he said—and for a breath his lips shaped the start of a prayer he hadn't spoken since childhood. But there was no god in Elsinore. Only servers.

The ghost surged forward, glitching so violently that its form split and stitched back together mid-frame.

"Avenge my murder."

The air stilled.

Harrow blinked. "Murder?"

The ghost hissed, its voice broken into metallic shards.

"Murder most foul. Most unnatural."

Harrow's jaw locked. "Tell me."

The ghost let out a mirthless laugh.

It shouldn't have been able to. But it did anyway. A dry, rasping sound—glitchy and unnatural.

"They say I broke. That the pressure shattered me. That I leapt."

The glitching intensified, and light flickered across its surface.

"Lies."

The air pushed down. The static turned physical.

"The serpent that killed me," it said, "now wears my crown."

Silence fell.

Harrow said the name like a curse. "Viktor."

Then again, harsher. "Viktor."

"He corrupted what you built," Harrow said, voice sharpening. "Turned legacy into leverage."

"Yes," the ghost rasped. "That smiling virus. Moved fast."

It glitched, its body blurring before stabilizing again.

"He wormed into my systems. Subtle. Surgical. Then…"

The voice dropped. "He pushed me."

Harrow stood frozen, every muscle coiled. "I suspected."

The ghost dimmed as it drifted closer.

"You must act. Elsinore is his now. The contracts. The data I locked down. He will weaponize it. The future will belong to him. Owned. Coded. Sealed."

"How?"

"He controls the substrate. He controls the AuRORA tech. I meant to remove despair from the population, to stop the rash of suicides during the war. Imagine what he can do with the tech now that I'm gone…"

Harrow gasped. With some coding, Viktor could control any emotion he chose to. He could sequester empathy in soldiers, block protesters from expressing outrage, override free will.

Behind the ghost, the city lights flickered like failing memories.

"He killed me without last rites," the ghost said. "I'm tormented. Bound to this purgatory."

Harrow's jaw tightened; dying without the sacraments was more than tragedy—it was exile.

"Spare your mother," it said, voice softening. "Let her live with the phantoms."

Its edges frayed. The light peeled away, each pixel of its form dissolving into nothingness, as if its code were dying. The mist swirled, thickening.

"Swear it," the ghost said.

Harrow didn't breathe.

"Swear it, Harrow."

Its face held. Almost human. Almost afraid.

"Audit the ledger, son. Trace the line from betrayal to execution. Balance it."

"I swear."

"Remember me."

And then it was gone.

No flash. No sound.

Absence.

Harrow stood in the darkness, the words etched into him like commands.

Avenge my murder.

The words ingrained themselves in Harrow's mind like code carved into flesh.

He didn't move. Didn't blink. Didn't breathe.

The world around him had vanished—only that voice remained, vibrating within him like a memory misfiled but never erased.

Then, quietly, he said, "So, uncle." The words barely left his lips, feeling like a blade sliding free of its sheath. His hands clenched as the cold pierced through his gloves, and he let it happen. "There you are."

He stepped closer to the edge, gazing down at the sprawling city below. The gala still shimmered beneath them—glass and chrome reflecting laughter programmed to distract from corpses.

"You murdered him," Harrow murmured. "Stole his crown. Claimed his wife. Took everything he was."

"I see you now."

Grief flickered inside him—brief, residual. Then gone.

This was the moment mourning ended, and the calculus of vengeance began.

Footsteps approached — fast, urgent — cutting through the stillness.

"Sir! Sir!"

Harrow turned smoothly and measuredly. A machine re-engaged.

Pax and Bjørn emerged from the mist, shapes coalescing from shadow and vapor.

Pax's eyes scanned him, concerned. "Are you alright?"

Bjørn looked stricken. "What happened?"

Harrow inhaled slowly, grounding himself. "A marvel," he said.

Pax took a cautious step forward. "Tell us."

But Harrow only shook his head. "You wouldn't believe me."

Then, after a beat: "Swear something to me."

The two men exchanged glances. Neither liked the sound of that.

"Never speak of what you saw tonight."

Silence stretched.

Then Pax nodded. "We swear."

Harrow didn't speak. He drew his dagger instead—sleek, real, thrumming with faint static.

He held it out between them, an oath waiting to be sealed—as solemn as any altar vow.

"Swear it," he said, "on this."

Bjørn hesitated.

And then the rooftop itself seemed to vibrate—a low, electric hum, as if the building's bones were beginning to resonate.

From the mist, a voice followed: "*Swear.*"

Neither human nor machine. A force on the spine. A command from nowhere and everywhere.

Bjørn flinched. "What was that?"

Harrow's eyes didn't waver. "He's still here."

He extended the blade again. Its light pulsed faintly.

"Swear it."

Pax reached out first. Steady. Certain. His hand touched the hilt.

Bjørn followed more slowly. His fingers trembled as they brushed the metal.

"We swear," they said.

And again, faint and echoing: "*Swear.*"

Then the rooftop went quiet. The hum subsided.

Silence settled in like judgment.

Harrow sheathed the dagger. The click echoed in the dark, sharp and final.

"Now…" he said, exhaling. "Let's go."

The moment shattered, and reality returned—music rose from below, lights sparkled through the mist, and the manufactured joy of the city remained undisturbed.

They turned to leave.

But Harrow heard none of it. His thoughts had already split into blueprints and possibilities, into names, paths, and contingencies.

There were things to do. Wrongs to right. Truths to reveal.

The ghost spoke, and he walked away. For the first time since the funeral, he knew exactly what he had to do.

CHAPTER 4

"Intimacy is a breach vector. Contain before compromise."

—SECURITY MEMO: VULNERABILITY MAPPING v4.1

In the morning, Harrow moved quietly through the hallway, each step slow, heavy, and deliberate. The overhead lights hummed softly, casting cold shadows across the polished floor. The sterile smell of filtered air and synthetic lilies clung to everything.

He hadn't slept. He hadn't even tried.

After the rooftop, after the ghost, after the oath—he'd paced for hours, back and forth across the floor of his flat. His thoughts refused to settle. Every time he closed his eyes, he saw his father's face—fractured and glitching, impossible to hold—and heard that final, cracking whisper: remember me.

He hadn't buttoned his shirt properly. His coat hung open, half-on and half-falling. His hair stuck out in uneven tufts from hours of raking his fingers through it. His AuRORAs had started pulsing warnings around 3:00 AM—heart rate elevated, adrenal spikes inconsistent—but he'd silenced them. He didn't need another voice telling him something was wrong.

He needed her.

He paused in front of Cassandra's door, hesitating as he stared at it—unsure whether to knock or walk away. His thumb brushed unconsciously over the small cross on his bracelet—a nervous habit from childhood—as if the metal could steady him.

Softly, he knocked.

There was a pause. A hesitation on the other side.

The door opened with a hush.

Cassandra stood in the doorway, her expression initially unreadable. When she saw him, something in her eyes lit up—perhaps relief—but it disappeared almost instantly. Her gaze swept over him, noticing the wildness, the disarray, and the silence.

"Harrow," she said, a small intake of breath. "What's happened?"

He didn't answer.

He stepped forward.

His hands rose slowly, as if moving through water, and he cupped her face with trembling fingers. She stiffened—only for a moment—but didn't pull away. Then he kissed her.

Not out of hunger. Not out of possession. Just desperate and silent.

Somewhere deep in his mind, the words of the old prayer rose and fell, unspoken, between one heartbeat and the next.

Cassandra made a quiet sound, almost a protest. Then she let herself lean in.

When he pulled back, he didn't let go of her. He reached down, took her left hand in his, and intertwined their fingers. He turned her hand over in his.

The back of her hand brushed against his cheek.

She whispered, uncertain: "Harrow?"

He rested his forehead against hers. Eyes closed. Breathing slowly. Unsteady.

He looked at her hand again.

There should have been a ring. Platinum. Skyglass from Europa. Clean. Elegant. He had tucked it away in a drawer, waiting for the right moment.

There would be no right time now. No future.

She wouldn't forgive him for what was about to happen. She wouldn't understand, and he couldn't blame her.

Still holding her hand, he stepped back.

One pace. Then another.

He didn't look at her face. Just her hand. Her bare fingers.

For a moment, he imagined what it would mean to stand with her before an altar—any altar—and speak vows instead of walking away. The thought burned, then passed.

He let out a slow, shuddering breath.

Then he turned. No words. No explanations. Suddenly absent.

And walked away.

The door slid shut behind him. Soft. Irrevocable.

The Neon breathed like a wounded animal.

Harrow kept his hands jammed deep in his coat pockets, collar up against the chemical drizzle. The rain here wasn't rain—it was condensation runoff from the tower's upper levels, thick with cool-ant and street grime. Each drop caused a faint sting where it touched skin.

He walked. He thought. The ghost's voice echoed behind him like static on an old comm line. *Remember me. Avenge my murder.* Words already fading, fragile as glass. Maybe it hadn't been real. Maybe the AuRORA had glitched. Or maybe grief was finally rot-ting his mind. He couldn't tell anymore.

The street opened into one of the Neon's wider arteries, where the wreckage from the Substrate War was still visible if you knew where to look. Apartment blocks patched together from bombed-out barracks. Rusted scaffolds leaning against walls pocked by shrapnel. Entire buildings bore scorch-shadows, outlines of people burned into concrete when the bombs exploded. The old relay towers still protruded from the skyline—angled, cracked, stripped of func-tion—like the ribs of something long dead.

Down on the ground, the crowd gathered. The city's poorest collected like runoff in a gutter. Holo-ads buzzed across broken screens, slogans glitching between corporate orders and wartime propaganda—*BE PRODUCTIVE / BE OBEDIENT / REMEM-BER THE ENEMY*—until the words bled together, meaningless.

Protesters clustered beneath them, drenched yet steadfast. Hand-painted signs bobbed on lengths of scavenged pipe.

"My body, not your firewall."

"Life isn't consent."

"Liberate AuRORA."

Their chants echoed unevenly, but the rage remained constant, like a drumbeat against the corporate silence.

Harrow stopped. Watched them.

They looked exhausted—eyes sunken, cheeks hollow—but they burned with a desperation that made his throat tighten. Mothers with children clutched them close, veterans with alloy limbs still sparking at the joints, kids no older than he'd been when the war ended and his father coded the first line of divine law. All of them stripped of the same thing: the right to decide how their lives should end.

The AuRORA ensured that. A kill-switch locked against the flesh. Mercy coded into circuitry, but mercy with a leash.

Harrow reflected on the ghost once more, on the accusation: *The serpent that killed me now wears my crown.*

Maybe the dead could lie. Maybe his mind could conjure phantoms to justify the violence he already wanted. But as he stared at the protesters shouting themselves hoarse in the Neon rain, framed by the ruins of a war fought over the very substrate that powered their chains, Harrow knew one thing was true—no one in this city owned their body anymore. Not them, not him.

Not even the ghost.

CHAPTER 5

"Affection is permissable only when monitored. Unwatched affection skews outcomes."

—FAMILY OVERSIGHT MANUAL: INTERNAL USE ONLY

Later that morning, Director Marr sat behind his security console, a sleek, minimalist alloy slab—an unspoken symbol of control and power. It reflected Elsinore Analytics' security division perfectly— cold, precise, unyielding, and designed to intimidate visitors that had no business there. Before unlocking the console that morning, Marr touched the small bronze medallion he kept in his inner pocket — not out of sentiment, but habit. A campaign token from the Substrate War, awarded to those who'd survived the siege at Novastadt. He never displayed it, never spoke of it, but his fingers still knew every worn groove. An old prayer ran through his head as his fingers brushed the worn relief, a ritual as private as it was precise.

The office walls were bare. Nothing sentimental. No personal touches. An intentional void where any curiosity went unanswered. Outside, far below the tower's soundproof glass, protesters still camped in the avenues, their chants reduced to a low, rhythmic tremor in the steel. Marr had grown used to it—the city's background noise, as easy to ignore as the wind—but he logged every face, every movement, every chant the same way he logged everything: as data waiting to be useful.

Dim lighting from a large holographic interface hovering above Marr's desk bathed the room. Pulsating—alive and always watching. Streams of data flowed across the display, intricate patterns demanded obscene pay for analysts who could decipher meaning from chaos. This constant flicker cast Marr's lined face into a menacing mask, a shadow puppet of corporate malice. He didn't mind—fear was as effective a management tool as competence, and usually easier.

With practiced theatricality, he swiped through the interface and encrypted the files. Digital locks cascaded shut in rapid succession, each click soft and decisive—secrets locked beyond reach. It was excessive security, even paranoid, but paranoia was Marr's currency. The war had taught him that systems often collapsed from the inside first. He'd carried that lesson into peacetime, turned it into doctrine. Zero trust.

He lifted his gaze, fixing it sharply on Reynaldo, who stood stiffly at attention, shoulders squared under the weight of expectations. Reynaldo was young enough to still believe that merit guaranteed advancement. Director Marr almost felt pity for him.

"Deliver these directly to Rook," Marr said, sliding the data shard across the desk's smooth surface with a mechanical motion.

The shard glimmered faintly under the room's ambient lighting, its biometric pass reflecting the light like a fine blade. Thin. Elegant. Lethal.

"No intermediaries," he said. "Understand?"

He made the sign of the cross over the shard—a motion so quick and subtle it could be mistaken for brushing away dust—as if sealing its contents under something more binding than encryption.

Reynaldo hesitated.

Only for a second—but that was all it took.

Marr's gaze held him in place. The air seemed heavier. His eyes didn't flash; there was no need. He watched, assessed, and saved the moment for later analysis.

Reynaldo swallowed and then straightened up to attention.

"Yes, sir," he said, his voice clipped and professional. He knew he'd been handed something radioactive, but he also understood there was no way to refuse.

Director Marr leaned back slowly, his fingers interlaced with clinical precision. His suit softly brushed against the chair. Tailored for silence. Built to conceal scars. His face showed no emotion.

He knew *exactly* what was on that drive.

Knew how many layers he'd built into the encryption.

Knew how many lives could be ruined—or erased—by the data contained within.

And he knew *exactly* whose hands it was meant to reach.

Reynaldo was simply the delivery system. Loyal. Discreet. *Expendable.*

"Move quickly," Marr said, his voice soft, almost gentle. "Time is sensitive."

He leaned forward, resting his elbows on the desk—just enough to shift the balance of power and make Reynaldo feel small. His eyes narrowed—not out of anger, but with focus. He didn't blink.

"Do not make me question your reliability."

That was everything. No threats. No raised voices. Just a quiet promise of consequences.

Reynaldo nodded again—sharper this time. "Understood."

Marr reached for another file.

There were more pieces to move.

"And after you deliver it," Director Marr said, voice level, "get me intel."

He slid a new file across the console. A secondary directive, untagged, non-networked. *Off-record.*

"Neo-Paris. I want to know who's there, what they're doing, and who they're afraid of. Map affiliations. Personal habits. Weaknesses."

Reynaldo stayed perfectly still. His face showed no change. But Marr had spent his life watching for tiny signs—and he caught the slight pause, the barely noticeable hitch in breath that always came before the internal question: *Why me?*

Marr smiled as if he'd already expected the objection. "And if my son's name surfaces—get very interested."

Reynaldo nodded once, a soldier's nod. Resigned to a grim errand.

"Understood, sir."

Director Marr leaned back, his hands steepled, embodying the quiet geometry of command. He observed Reynaldo with algorithmic calm—ten moves ahead. Once, during the Substrate War, he'd run infiltration cells with the same precision: map the outer ring, find a small vulnerability, infect, collapse the center.

"Be subtle," he said. "Do not appear to be asking questions. Introduce his name casually—a further thread in a conversation you're not fully committed to. They'll fill in the rest."

He paused. Let that sink in.

"Drop a line like, 'Rook? Think I ran into him once at a gallery or a gambling den. Seemed sharp.' Not too polished. Not too vague. Just enough static to make people want to clarify.

"People correct lies faster than they confess truths," he said, eyes narrowing. "Especially when they think they're smarter than you."

Reynaldo shifted. "Suggest something … questionable?"

Director Marr's voice dropped an octave.

"Hint. Don't accuse. Let the idea of vice linger—unspoken but undeniable. Late nights. High bets. Unlicensed codework. Nothing criminal, nothing provable. Just enough to make the people around him wonder what else they *don't* know."

He paused. Then, casually:

"You'll know you've succeeded if they start defending him."

Reynaldo's brows knit, his unease visible now. "That won't damage his—"

"Reputation?" Director Marr cut in. "It's not his reputation I'm monitoring. It's the people around him."

He rose, slowly, voice gaining the weight of doctrine.

"A network is only as secure as its weakest link—usually the outer ring because they don't know they hold any secrets. And Rook

… Rook doesn't think he has a network. That's the most dangerous kind of naivety."

Reynaldo looked away. "Yes, sir."

Director Marr watched him for another few seconds. Not speaking. Simply *evaluating*.

Then, smoothly: "You may go."

Reynaldo hesitated—only for a beat—then left, the sound of the door sliding shut as quiet as the tension he left behind.

Marr didn't trust Rook. But more importantly, he didn't trust what Rook *might become*.

He turned back to his console. A map of Neo-Paris flickered on the display—territories, profiles, tagged faces. A slow build. Quiet patterns emerged.

The door slid open with its usual mechanical hiss.

Cassandra stepped inside, pale and shaken, her eyes wide with the same panic that usually follows a tragedy. Her breath was uneven, and her fingers twitched at her sides, as if she didn't know what to do with them.

Marr looked up from his console, his face a mix of annoyance, concern, and calculation. Then, smoothly standing, he crossed the room to meet her.

"Cassandra?" His voice was sharp and controlled. "What's wrong?"

She didn't reply right away. When she finally did, it felt like her breath was struggling out of tight lungs.

"Father," she said, "he … Harrow. He came to me. Just showed up."

Director Marr's jaw tightened. "When?"

"Less than an hour ago."

His eyes narrowed—not in surprise, but in confirmation. The timestamp matched the feed.

"Did he say anything?"

She hesitated. "No. He looked … strange. Disconnected. His jacket was hanging open, implants off. Like he wasn't even *in* the system anymore."

Director Marr nodded once and stepped back to his desk. He tapped something beneath the surface. On the screen behind him, silent and grainy, the security feed flickered: Harrow in the corridor. Harrow entering her flat. Harrow leaving. All time-stamped. All archived.

He didn't let her see it. Not yet.

"Go on," he said, tone unreadable.

"He was … shaken. His hair was wild, like he hadn't slept. He grabbed my hand, stared at me, like I was—" her voice faltered "—like I was the only thing still real to him."

Her eyes dropped. "He didn't speak. Just held me. And then he left."

Director Marr studied her.

Silence. Not heavy. *Tense.* Like a string being drawn slowly between two sharp points.

And then—softly—

"You're leaving something out."

Cassandra's head snapped up. Her eyes widened.

Director Marr remained still. He made no accusations. His voice did not rise. He gently touched the edge of the desk, once.

"I have security clearance, Cassandra. I know exactly how long he was there. I know what the motion sensors registered."

He let that hang in the air.

"I know he kissed you."

Cassandra flinched. Not from shame. From being *violated*.

"What difference does it make?"

Director Marr sighed heavily and disappointedly. He had established boundaries, and she had crossed them.

"I taught you better than this," he said. "If you're going to omit, make it plausible. Don't waste my time with half-truths. Not now."

Her voice was tight, brittle. "I didn't lie."

"You withheld," he said.

Cassandra looked away, jaw clenched. "I didn't know what to say."

He stepped closer, lowering his voice. "Next time, offer the whole truth or offer nothing. The truth becomes a lie when you obscure the details."

Another pause.

Marr turned back to the console and opened a different window, with code flowing past in a silent cascade.

"He's unraveling," he said. "And if he spirals in public, it becomes *our* crisis."

She didn't respond.

Marr shut the feed down with a swipe. "I'll inform Viktor."

Cassandra blinked. "You're reporting him?"

"I'm protecting you," he said. "And the company. Elsinore can't afford an heir heading toward a nervous breakdown. His grief is a deficit. If we don't intervene, it'll trigger an audit at the worst possible time."

She swallowed everything she wanted to say.

He gave her one last glance. Not cruel. Not warm. *Closed.*

"Go home," he said. "Get some sleep. Say nothing."

Marr logged the encounter with the same precision he logged everything: a variable to monitor, nothing more. Then he reached for the next file. There was always another file.

CHAPTER 6

"Augmented Reality Optical Relay Algorithm (AuRORA) modules
must not be rebooted during memory review procedures."

—ELSINORE SYSTEMS OVERSIGHT MANUAL, SECTION 12.4.1

On Monday morning, eyes shifted toward Viktor even before the
drones announced his arrival. His fingers formed a steeple on the
table, tapping once—as punctuation to a thought he hadn't spoken.
The gesture lingered a beat too long, almost like a man about to begin
prayer—a private liturgy of power. His bone-white nano-weave suit
shimmered, reflecting the light. He looked calm and confident,
engaging in small talk and smiling warmly. Unthreatening. But
beneath that calm, a coil of cold, calculating, and ruthless violence
lurked. A man who could erase you like a clerical error.

Beside him sat Corra. She projected an air of practiced calm.
Her tone was soft and reassuring. But her posture was stiff, revealing her unease. Viktor chuckled, but she didn't blink. Her fingers

remained too still, and her eyes lingered on Viktor's reflection in the glass a moment longer than necessary. Her gaze didn't flinch under Viktor's glance, but her fingers subtly drifted, almost involuntarily, to the faint scar beneath her cuff.

Behind them, the cybernetic aides hummed softly—drones analyzing data at incredible speeds. They moved with respect, like priests tending to a digital deity. Privacy, here, was not extinct. It had never existed.

What mattered was narrative. What mattered was control.

Viktor Eisler was born into the wrong half of the family. Second son. Second place. The company was never his, not really. Elsinore Analytics had already chosen its heir: Silas. Firstborn. Prodigy. Golden boy with a compiler for a brain. The Substrate War only widened the gap—Silas, the wartime savior, with his divine firewall; Viktor, the brother left standing in the smoke, with nothing but resentment.

Viktor learned early what that meant. No matter how sharp his instincts, no matter how steady his hand, he'd always be the spare. Silas wrote elegant code. Viktor read people—and broke them if he had to. Leadership came naturally. But leadership didn't matter when inheritance was already signed in blood.

The brothers fought over everything: school scores, internships, scraps of approval at the boardroom table. They pushed each other past the breaking point, and still Viktor came away empty. You couldn't outwit birthright. You couldn't outplay a system wired for someone else.

And then came Corra. Silas married her—another prize he

didn't earn. Viktor smiled at the wedding, raised his glass, played the loyal brother. Inside, he was seething. He never stopped.

By the time Elsinore handed Silas the crown, Viktor had stopped pretending. Genius wasn't the same as vision. Programming wasn't the same as power. The company needed a leader, not a dreamer, and he was the only one that understood that. The war had proven as much: code didn't win sieges, leaders did. Soldiers followed vision, not syntax

Second son or not, Viktor knew the truth. The legacy should have been his.

He tapped once on the table.

Scene cue.

The doors hissed open.

Keir Tavant entered, flanked by two silent, angular security drones.

Harrow's former companion. Now, the courier for corporate interests. His suit was flawless—threaded with nanotech shimmer. But the way he stood, shoulders slouched and head bowed, gave him away.

Viktor stood.

"Keir," Viktor said, smiling just enough. "Our prince is unraveling. Existential itch he can't scratch?"

Corra exhaled softly, nearly inaudible. Her grip on the stem of the glass she wasn't drinking from tightened.

"He's withdrawn," she said. "He's avoiding everyone. Staring through walls, daring them to blink first."

Viktor ignored her, keeping his eyes on Keir.

"We'd like you to reach out. Nothing overt. Just proximity. See what he says. What he avoids. Who he thinks about."

Keir gave a quick nod. "Of course. I'll keep it casual. Ease in."

Viktor gestured to an aide nearby. "Take him to Harrow's suite. See if our prince is meditating on mortality or market volatility."

As Keir turned to leave, Corra spoke. Not loud. But pleading. "Please."

He turned back. Her voice carried weight beyond concern. It carried fear.

"Help him," she said.

Keir nodded, but his smile had faded. He was about to face someone he had called a friend, but who might now be a liability.

The drones followed him out.

The door hissed shut.

Viktor exhaled. "Now we wait."

The temperature shifted. The glass-and-steel room shimmered with neon reflections—like a shrine dressed in cold steel.

Viktor turned to Bjørn, who stood patiently by the door. "You have news concerning the protesters?"

"Yes, sir," said Bjørn. "We've identified a leader of sorts. Jessica Hvit. Lives in the Neon and works as a custodian."

"Find her," Viktor said. "And neutralize her."

The door hissed again.

Director Marr entered. Tailored coat. Balanced stride. Every move was efficient. Polished. He was a man built for utility, not legacy.

The first time Viktor met Marr, the man didn't look like much—

single father, secondhand suit, unrefined but with sharp eyes. But he carried himself with the lean patience of a veteran—a man who'd crawled through the Substrate War's ruins and learned the value of clear intel and of judicious silence. Marr had this way of listening. No overt questions, just the suggestion of shared knowledge. Information clung to him, drawn out of others as if by gravity. By the time the meeting ended, Viktor realized he hadn't hired an informant. He'd recruited a predator.

Viktor didn't rise. His lenses dimmed as he scanned Marr before the man spoke.

"Sir," Marr said, tone flat. "I believe I've found the source of Harrow's behavioral collapse."

Viktor's interest sharpened. "Finally. Something real."

Marr smiled, no warmth. "My loyalty is absolute."

Viktor nodded. "And your talent for survival is remarkable."

Marr sat. Steepled fingers.

"His neural patterns match stimulant withdrawal. Obsession loops. Cortisol spikes. He's not grieving. He's unraveling on a romantic variable."

Viktor's gaze darkened. "You're telling me this collapse is over a woman?"

Marr didn't blink. "I'm telling you Harrow's addicted to someone who stopped supplying."

Viktor's expression didn't flicker. "Romantic dysfunction?"

"It fits the pattern."

Corra finally spoke. "We're aware of the variables. His father. Our marriage. Succession pressure."

Marr waved it away. "Static. The signal is clearer."

He produced a datapad.

"Exhibit A."

A stylized scan of Harrow's handwriting.

He read aloud: "To my beloved … Doubt thou the stars are fire…"

He let the silence bloom.

Corra leaned forward. "He wrote this?"

"To Cassandra," Marr said. "Weeks ago. She gave it to me when she saw how far he was slipping. I told her to cut him off."

Viktor frowned. "And you think rejection did this?"

"I know it did. Rejection corrodes. Especially when you're raised in a sphere of entitlement."

Viktor folded his arms. "Prove it."

Marr tapped the interface. The screen flickered into focus: Harrow in the atrium, pacing in figure-eights. Ocular HUD darkened. Neural sync faint. He paused occasionally to touch objects he'd already passed—like testing for reality.

"Insert Cassandra," Marr said. "Let her speak to him. Unscripted. Observed. If he reacts, we confirm everything."

Viktor nodded. "Do it."

Corra remained still, her eyes fixed on the screen.

"He's still mourning," she said. "He doesn't know how."

Neither man responded.

Marr stood up and quickly turned away. He left the conference room without saying another word.

Affection was vulnerability. And he knew how to patch it.

Corra's eyes didn't leave the screen. After Marr had left, she spoke again—quietly this time. "Are you sure this is the best idea?"

Viktor didn't respond, having already turned away and mumbled something to a nearby aide—as if Corra's voice had glitched out entirely.

Corra frowned. "I just think—"

"Yes," Viktor said. "We know what you think."

She looked away, toward the floor-to-ceiling windows. Far below, protesters still clustered at the base of the tower, their banners snapping in the wind. From this height, their chants were just vibrations against the glass, swallowed by the hum of the drones. Elsinore City kept pulsing beyond them, indifferent to her own aching heart. Her fingers brushed the small pendant at her collar—a gesture so practiced it was no longer belief, only habit—and she whispered something soundless to the glass.

CHAPTER 7

"Sincerity is discouraged. Scripted responses are more reliable."

—EMOTIONAL INTEGRITY DIRECTIVE, PUBLIC-FACING PERSONNEL v3.1

Harrow stood by the towering glass window in the Elsinore atrium. The city's neon flickered in the glass—like veins under synthetic skin. Electric pink and corporate blue danced across his face's contours, shaping him into something stretched and haunted—less a man than a mood the building couldn't shake off. The atrium glass itself was part of a reconstruction contract inked in the war's ash; everything here wore the Substrate War in its seams, whether it admitted it or not.

Beyond the glass, protesters packed the street in ragged rows, their signs bobbing like buoys in a churning sea. They'd been there since the death of Silas Eisler—day and night, through rain that slicked the asphalt and heat that turned the air into a smear of static. It wasn't that they wanted to die; they wanted the right to choose, to breach the divine firewall on their own terms. The slogans flickered on smart-fabric banners: *"My life, my exit." "Root access for all."* The cadence was inherited from the Substrate War ration lines—the old chant patterns of people who learned to survive by the ritual.

Harrow stood watching, forehead almost against the glass. Sometimes he felt the pull—felt the itch in his hands to leave the tower, to join them in the crush and noise, to lift a sign and shout until his voice broke. Not because he wanted to die, but because standing still inside these walls felt like a slow suicide.

The holobook in his hands pulsed gently, its pages shimmering and threatening to dissolve into static, with a faint electric scent accompanying its data as it struggled to stay intact. The book mimicked reality but lacked the comforting weight, the distinctive smell of aged paper and ink, and the familiar texture of legitimate wisdom. Instead, it was legacy code from an earlier world, repackaged in Elsinore's proprietary format. Half its text came from pre-war archives that survived the blackout months. Scarred texts patched and recompiled to make them presentable. The words hovered between lines of encryption, softly whispering Shakespearean tragedy recompiled for a boardroom audience.

He turned a page. The system lagged. A glitch flickered across the page, then disappeared—Cassandra's name. He stared at the blank space on the screen where the words should have appeared, a digital silence intensifying his feelings of displacement.

Harrow paced steadily, not restless or melodramatic. This was something quieter, controlled, and clinical—a machine running diagnostics and constantly coming up red. The book—his father's, perhaps, or a replica Viktor had given him for PR optics—served only as a prop in the ritual now. He wasn't reading it; he was measuring his own decline by how little of it remained.

Outside, the city flashed with a thousand advert screens screaming a pitch to buy, upgrade, or consume. Inside, Harrow stood motionless, breathing through clenched teeth, his eyes dull with calculation. In another life, he might have been a philosopher. Here, he was either an asset or a liability waiting to be monetized or liquidated.

The door gently hissed open as Director Marr entered the somber atrium.

His footsteps echoed loudly against the polished floor—each one a sharp punctuation mark in a space meant for silence. The overhead lights shone too brightly, casting a glare off every surface. Somewhere deep within the walls, a processor fan whined. It was the same thin, metallic note the substrate generators used to make when neighborhoods were running on fumes.

"Sir," Director Marr said, voice clipped.

Harrow didn't rise. He sat hunched on a low bench beneath a cracked monitor, his face washed pale by a flickering feed. In his hands lay a digital codex, sleek and archaic—half relic, half weaponized affectation.

"Director Marr," Harrow said tonelessly. "Tell me—running side hustles now? Selling code by the kilo?"

"No, sir." Marr's reply was flat, automatic.

"Shame." Harrow thumbed a page. Blue text shimmered, crawling over his cheekbones like circuitry. "Hackers at least admit they're thieves. Honesty. Scarce resource these days."

"Honesty," Marr repeated, without inflection.

"Extinct, more like."

Silence stretched. Marr held it without strain, his hands still behind his back, implant light steady.

"What are you reading, sir?" he asked at last.

Harrow lifted the codex listlessly, eyes flicking over the glow. "Noise."

"Noise?"

"Loops. Commands strutting as if they mean something." His voice pitched louder. "Words, Director. Just words."

Marr waited.

"Words," Harrow said again, slower, as if speaking to a defective interface.

Nothing from Marr. Not a twitch.

"What is it about?" he prompted.

Harrow snapped the codex shut. The sound cracked the air. "Satire. Says here old men run on obsolete firmware, their optics glitch, memory corrupt. Nothing but legacy code rotting in the system." His gaze cut up, sudden and precise. "Does that sound familiar?"

Marr didn't blink. "That is one reading."

The silence pressed close, buzzing faintly with static. Harrow tilted his head, studying Marr, as if trying to provoke some crack in the façade.

He found none.

"Your implant is overdue for recalibration, sir. Shall we run the scan now?"

Harrow's laugh cracked sharp and brittle. "You'd like that, wouldn't you? Peel me open. See if the ghost inside rattles when you shake the frame."

Marr didn't move. "Data doesn't lie, sir. People do."

He turned and walked away silently.

Harrow watched him go. Didn't move.

The atrium was quiet now, except for the low thrum of city power pulsing through the walls. Neon faintly seeped through the window, casting shifting reflections across the black floor. Harrow watched the old man; a bitter smile crossed his lips—weak and brief, like failing neon.

"Fucking fools," he said, the words barely audible beneath the weight pressing down on him—grief, paranoia, memory.

The security locks disengaged with a quiet hiss, and the doors slid open to reveal Keir—briefly flanked by the pulsing blue gaze of a retinal scanner and the soft beep of identity confirmation.

He entered cautiously.

His suit was sharp—top-tier corporate cut, shoulders square, implants barely visible beneath the collar—but his face felt off. A bit too smooth. A little too calculated. Rehearsed warmth.

"Hey, Harry!" Keir said, voice a half-step too bright.

Harrow turned slowly, rising from the bench as if he were waking from sleep. His eyes followed him with the wariness of someone who had expected him—but hoped he might be wrong.

He grinned, flashing teeth and a hint of weariness. "Ah, my

favorite operative. What brings you to this delightful corner of the dystopian panopticon?"

Keir gave the atrium a once-over. "Not exactly the Ritz, but not the gutter either."

Harrow shrugged. "Same difference. Both charge more than they're worth."

Their laughter, a fragile, echoing sound, resembled static—thin and wispy in the air, like the faintest wisp of smoke. The overhead lights flickered, and one of the security drones briefly pivoted before resuming its orbit. Old surveillance chassis from the war years still did their rounds here, repainted and leased new names.

"You're fucking impossible," Keir said with a friendly voice. He shuffled his feet.

"Only when necessary," Harrow shot back, eyes glinting like cracked glass. "But tell me—what crime lands you in my particular cell block of this corporate prison?"

"Prison?" Keir raised a brow.

"Elsinore's a prison, my friend," Harrow said, voice lower now. Less banter. More rot.

"Then the whole world's a prison," Keir said in a philosophical tone.

"A vast correctional complex," Harrow said. "Endless wings, hidden sectors, and too many inmates to count. But Elsinore? Solitary confinement, top-tier. Maximum security."

"I don't see it that way," Keir said, glancing up at the security camera blinking silently above the doorway.

"Ah, perception," Harrow said, smiling darkly. "The glitch in every system. For me, it's a cage. For you? A luxury suite."

"Maybe you just think too much," Keir offered.

"Guilty," Harrow said, voice frayed. "If my mind shut up, paradise might fit on a data shard."

There was a silence then, brief but sharp.

"Still haunted by bad dreams?" Keir asked.

"What is life," Harrow said, eyes fixed on the far-off city, "if not a waking nightmare in business-casual?"

Keir shrugged. "Dreams are just reflections. Noise in the buffer."

"Reflections of reflections," Harrow said, almost to himself. "Synthetic sunlight through glass in a windowless room."

He turned to Keir, suddenly animated, gesturing toward the skyline beyond the reinforced smart-glass. Neon writhed there like a dragon. Those same gridlines once rationed power block by block during the Substrate War; the city learned to glow around its scars.

"And yet—what if all this is just a dream we're coding together? A shared hallucination with good branding?"

The atrium fell quiet again. Too many things unsaid.

The lights buzzed overhead.

And somewhere, deeper in the building, the system kept recording.

The atrium's silence settled over them like dust—fine, invasive, impossible to ignore.

Above, the lights dimmed slightly, flickering like an anxious spasm in the building's neural net. Somewhere in the corner, one of the ceiling-mounted lenses adjusted its angle, emitting a soft whirr that Harrow pretended not to notice.

Keir shifted, the smile he offered cracking at the edges. "Too much philosophy for this hour. Let's go downtown."

Harrow's eyes, dark and unblinking, gleamed like glass slick with rain. "At my disposal, are you?"

"Of course," Keir said.

"Never," Harrow said. "You're a spy with a side hustle as a friend."

Keir flinched. "That's harsh," he said, but he didn't deny it. His fingers twitched restlessly near the seam of his coat—an old reflex, part muscle memory and part guilt. In that moment, he looked like he longed for the comfort of simpler times.

"Is it?" Harrow leaned in, his voice dropping to something lower, private. "They're watching me. They're watching you. Fun, huh?"

That shut him up.

The room seemed to hum louder, as if it agreed.

Harrow reclined, stretching slightly as if the tension hadn't ingrained itself into every inch of his spine. He waved to summon drinks—sleek black cylinders slid across the table, their contents hissing softly as the temperature equalized. "Let's pretend we're free men," he said in a bright tone.

They sat. Or tried to. Neither fully relaxed.

"Why are you here?" Harrow asked, voice flat.

"To see you," Keir said. The words tumbled out, rehearsed and smooth.

"Liar." Harrow grinned, all teeth and venom. "Who sent you?"

Keir didn't speak. But his silence made plenty of noise.

"Did you come freely?" Harrow pressed, his gaze sharp and unwavering, a subtle smirk playing on his lips as he waited for the inevitable.

Keir sighed. "I was sent for."

"Of course," Harrow said, as if that proved anything. He leaned back again, his face a mask of exhaustion that didn't care about being believed. "Here's the plot twist: I already know. My joy's gone. The world's a cheap set piece. That sky?" He pointed up at the smart-glass above them. "Just a toxic ceiling pretending to be the stars."

The room held still. Afraid to interrupt him.

"Man," Harrow said, "a creature of reason, reduced to dust chasing false gods."

"You've lost interest in everything," Keir said, watching him closely now.

"Shocking," Harrow said, dry and empty. "No joy in fools."

A silence settled again. Leaving the two men alone, even as the walls recorded every breath.

Suddenly, the blare of Elsinore's alert system echoed through the atrium, sharp and metallic—a proximity ping signaling an access request.

"Entertainment," Keir said from across the table, startled by the noise. "I found some actors and booked them for Friday. They must have arrived to look over the performance space."

Harrow's attention snapped into focus. Something bright surged behind his tired eyes. "Actors," he said, almost reverently. "Honest liars in a dishonest world."

The atrium doors swung open, unleashing a wave of vibrant costumes, pulsing music, and excited chatter that flooded the room. Static clung to their movements, charged by the city's energy and their own relentless momentum. They wore tattered coats and high-tech gear that fell short of company standards. Misfits. Nomads. Artists. Some of their kit was obvious war-surplus—optics housings with old registry stamps sanded down, field-batteries re-sleeved for theater light.

Harrow stepped forward to meet them. His smile was genuine this time, with no hint of calculation; it was raw and sincere. He gripped the lead player's arm firmly, his knuckles turning white, as if anchoring himself to the moment.

"Did the protesters give you a hard time coming through?" Keir asked, his tone edged with contempt.

"No, no," the stage manager said, brushing dust from his sleeves. "They were kind enough."

"Their picketing is ridiculous," Keir muttered, shaking his head.

"Do you honestly think that, Keir?" Harrow released the actor's arm and stepped forward, eyes narrowing. "You don't want control of your life?"

The stage manager hesitated, cleared his throat, and looked down. "I remember the suicides," he said at last. His voice had the weary cadence of someone revisiting old scars. "I remember the desperation after the Substrate War. We all understand why your father did it, why he created the divine firewall. But the protesters are right. Your father is—was—a hypocrite."

Keir surged forward, bristling. "How dare—"

"It's okay, Keir." Harrow's voice cut clean through the tension. He held his friend's gaze for a moment, then turned back to the stage manager. "Sometimes the truth is sharp and painful."

The silence that followed wasn't empty. It was charged. Harrow's mind flickered, restless—ghost images, half-formed notions threading together. And then it struck him: theater. An old performance, a man murdering his brother for power.

He could see it already—actors moving under hot lights, words rising like smoke, the story laid bare before an audience who thought it was entertainment. And at the center of that audience, Viktor. Watching. Trapped. If guilt lived in him, it would show. A twitch, a wince, a crack in the polished veneer. And Harrow would know.

He would know, and then he would act.

"Prepare *The Murder of Claudius*," Harrow said. His voice was steady, deliberate, the decision sealing itself as he spoke. "And I'll add a few lines of my own."

The stage manager's eyes flicked upward, studying him for a beat. Then he nodded once. "Of course."

When they left, the spark disappeared from Harrow's face. His grin faded, his shoulders slumped, and he turned back to the city through the tall glass windows. Lights flickered like stars—bright enough to remind him of how far he had fallen.

Actors can fake anything: love, rage, tears.

He clenched his fists. He couldn't fake this.

He needed proof.

He needed a trap.

The whole thing is merely a play, a deadly melodrama, he thought, staring out at the stormy skyline of Elsinore. Beneath the glow of surveillance satellites and hollow towers, many of them war-era constellations repurposed for peacetime compliance, something cold and certain locked into place in his chest. And maybe, just maybe, he could finally do something about it—take the lead in this drama.

CHAPTER 8

"A consistent narrative is more important than truth. Delay invites scrutiny."

—Elsinore Communications Operations Manual, Messaging Prioritization Protocol v3.8

Late that night, Cassandra sat cross-legged on the floor, her back pressed against the couch, tablet balanced across her knees. The striplight above pulsed faintly like the building's heartbeat, but the glow from her screen was steadier, colder.

She rerouted her optic feed twice, then once more—not paranoia, precision. The blind spot was hers, carved weeks ago in a maintenance cycle Marr never checked. She had been waiting for the right moment to pull the thread. Tonight was the moment.

Onscreen: a draft message, unsent but stamped red priority, Marr to Viktor. Keywords blinked: "escalation," "containment," "asset drift," and—twice—"Harrow."

She skimmed the text. The body was noise. The metadata was the prize: routing chains, urgency codes, failure redundancies. Marr thought in contingencies, and contingencies required entry points. Every point she mapped was another stone in the quiet foundation she was laying—a network of fractures that one day would bring the Tower down from the inside.

Her lips quirked, almost a smile. She wasn't stealing information; she was building her war chest. She had spent months carefully probing for vulnerabilities—an unsecured port, a forgotten employee account, an unpatched server. She moved laterally through the network, testing every point of entry, every compromised device. She slowly escalated her privileges, carefully mimicking legitimate behavior. Now she had the keys needed to unleash an unstoppable weapon. A blade that could be wielded with the skill of a surgeon or thrust without mercy into the heart of the dragon.

A quiet tap. She duplicated the message, queued it for transmission, then inserted a two-stage loop in the routing algorithm: first a false success receipt, then a recursive latency flag that would reroute it through three proxy nodes and hold it for six hours. Maybe eight, depending on network traffic.

To Viktor, it would read as a spine-server hiccup. To Marr, it would pass unnoticed. To Harrow, it would vanish into silence. Three lies stacked together, and she balanced them like blades on her palm.

She stared at the screen a moment longer. Then she edited one word in the original message. Just one. "Intervene" became "observe."

Not much. Just enough.

She tapped the screen, shut the tablet, and slid it beneath the couch.

She stayed on the floor. The couch behind her gave a faint groan, as if weight shifted where there was none. From the hallway came the muffled hum of footsteps, then silence—too abrupt, as if someone had stopped to listen. Somewhere above, the automated vent clicked softly—a nervous tic in the wall. Below, a drone buzzed past the building on patrol, its motion sensors sweeping windows like fingers grazing glass. Further down, past the corporate checkpoints, the protest lines would be forming for the night—wet banners, stubborn chants. They still sang the war's old chants without knowing it—refrains carried down from parents who had survived on slogans when rations ran out. Cassandra pictured herself there, shoulder to shoulder with them, if her life allowed it. But here she was, locked in a gilded cage, watching from the wrong side of the glass.

Cassandra folded her arms around her knees. Her fingers brushed against the faint circle in her pocket—the Saint Expeditus coin Harrow had once left on her desk without explanation. She turned it over once, feeling the worn relief under her thumb, before tucking it away again.

Marr's words were clipped, bureaucratic, but she knew the subtext: "contain" meant erase. He'd perfected that diction during the Substrate War, when orders had to provide deniability. He never issued the same order twice. If this message reached Viktor unaltered, Harrow's window was already closing.

She rested her head against the wall and closed her eyes.

She'd kissed him. She had kissed him a million times before, but this time felt different. That was the part that wouldn't settle.

It looped in her mind like faulty code, replaying with imperfect recall—his breath, the trembling in his hands, her own damn hesitation. If it had just been a trick of grief, a trauma reflex, it should have faded by now. But it hadn't. It was still there. Still real.

She had kissed him.

And then she had altered a message that might have gotten him killed.

Not for love. Not even for loyalty.

Because she was tired of watching men like her father pretend they were playing chess while real people bled out on the board.

Cassandra drew her legs in more tightly, wrapping her arms around herself like a brace. Her bare feet rested on cold tile. No theater here. No audience.

Only choices. And consequences.

The worst part was, she didn't know if she was trying to save Harrow—

—or sabotage him on her own terms.

She remained curled up on the floor a little longer.

Then she uncoiled and crossed to the far corner of the room. There, behind the false panel in the wall, she withdrew a shard of old storage tech—outdated, obsolete, untraceable. The kind that had flooded black markets during the Substrate War, when networks collapsed and people hoarded whatever could still hold memory. A relic from the days before her father was Director Marr, before he dressed in protocols and hid behind policy.

She slotted the shard into the tablet.

No sync. No signal. No call-and-response handshake with the

cloud. Just the dull, satisfying click of independence.

She opened a dead inbox under a name no one remembered. The address had been scrubbed from her records years ago, but she still remembered the password.

The message loaded in pieces. Her falsified timestamp held. She added a second file—her version, with the edit—then a final note:

"Original and modified. In case memory falters."

She didn't sign it. If someone ever found it, it needed to speak for itself.

When it was done, she pulled out the shard, dropped it back into the hollow space behind the wall, and pressed the panel shut.

She stood in the quiet for a while.

Not watching the city. Not making speeches in her mind. She stood in the quiet. The silence felt staged, rehearsed, like the room was holding its breath. Survival was possible, maybe. But not clean. Not on her terms.

CHAPTER 9

"Loyalty is a liability when applied outside approved parameters."

—Tactical Ethics Module, Field Deployment Manual v4.3

The rain in Neo-Paris didn't fall—it hovered. Suspended mist, charged with static and the taste of old wars. Rook pulled his collar higher and moved through the back alleys. His coat was military issue, cut down and resewn so it wouldn't draw attention. The black had faded to bruised graphite. Scorch marks stitched the hem. It had been issued in the last year of the Substrate War, when new uniforms had to be stitched together faster than the dead could be buried. He'd stopped cleaning it months ago. Made it look less like armor. More like history.

The street-level façade of the city was all chrome and charm. Holo-displays looped curated advertisements with soothing voices and tailored dopamine hits. But down here—beneath the storefronts and respectability—was where the city exhaled. Rust. Ozone.

Grease. Old blood. The underlayers of Rue Souterraine were lined with forgotten tech, buried servers still humming in concrete tombs, and repurposed exhaust tunnels breathing steam like dying dragons. Most of it had been jury-rigged during the war, when Neo-Paris kept its heart beating by splicing old networks onto scorched infrastructure.

No surveillance nodes down here. Or at least, none that made their presence known.

Kira's place was still exactly where he remembered—fourth hatch past the corroded mag-train corridor, nestled between a knockoff dermal-repair kiosk and a shuttered funeral printer that hadn't dispensed ashes in years. The hatch was matte black, pockmarked with arc burns, and etched at the corner with a sigil that predated code. It hummed faintly when his hand passed over it.

He knocked once. Twice. Waited. Then three sharp raps.

A click. A hiss. A sliver of light.

"You're late," came the voice.

"Didn't know I was expected."

"You're not. That's why you're late."

The hatch opened wider. He stepped through.

Inside, Kira's den smelled like overclocked processors and spilled synth-ink. It was dark, except for the screens—layered in every direction, some mounted, some hanging from wires, a few stacked on crates. They glowed with waves of green and violet, like a digital reef. The air crackled with interference.

Kira was hunched over a soldering table, one boot resting on a gear bin, her jacket sleeves rolled up to the elbows. Her arms were wiry, tattooed with outdated subroutines and coordinates no map recognized. Wires snaked through her sleeves like veins. She didn't look up when he entered.

"You always knock like a cop."

"You always answer like a fugitive."

"Some of us don't have corporate bloodlines to burn through."

Rook's lips twitched, almost forming a smile. He hadn't smiled in weeks.

She finally turned, raising one eyebrow. "You here for tea, whiskey, or plausible deniability?"

"Denial. Two sugars."

She poured whiskey. Same chipped cup as last time.

He didn't drink.

Kira was a veteran of the Substrate War, disillusioned when she saw governments and corporations spilling blood over substrate for AuRORA tech. If it had been for water or food, she might have understood. But people were dying for luxuries—for an easy life.

"So," she said after a long silence, "you going to tell me what kind of trouble you're in, or just keep pacing like an idiot?"

Rook stopped. Let out a breath. "I need a scrambler. Neural. Self-contained. Something clean. Something that won't melt my spine."

Kira whistled low. "Someone's paranoid."

"Someone has reason."

She crouched beside a half-assembled drone, pulled a stash from underneath it, and held up a coin-sized matte disc. "Self-erasing after two minutes. Blocks most mid-tier scans, but if Elsinore's running anything above Black Signal, it's just noise. This'll buy you a breath. Maybe two."

"I'll take it."

She tossed it. He caught it one-handed. Turned it over in his fingers. It looked innocuous. Like a toy. Like nothing.

Kira watched him. "They've got cameras in church pews now," she said. "Bio-readers in public drinking fountains. Surveillance as a sacrament. You think you're off-grid because you took a boat to Neo-Paris?"

"No one followed me."

She scoffed. "You don't leave the system, Rook. You just stop getting memos."

He looked away, eyes drifting to a screen looping silent footage—Elsinore Tower, distant and pristine. Protesters choked on tear gas. A flare ignited like a signal fire. Thick smoke hiding betrayal.

"They're serious, aren't they?" Kira asked.

Rook didn't answer.

"Good for them," she said. "The divine firewall is overkill."

Rook choked back a laugh.

"You going back?"

Rook let the silence stretch.

After a moment, she reached under the table and pulled out a second disc. This one wasn't smooth; it was jagged and scarred around the edge—like it had already survived something. She'd scavenged it from the warfront once, dug out of wreckage where an entire block's worth of memories had burned.

"For later," she said, handing it to him.

"I didn't ask for a second one."

"Didn't ask for the first either. Call it nostalgia."

Rook slipped both into a hidden pocket. The fabric was reinforced there. Military-grade. Some habits didn't break.

"Careful with that one," Kira said as he turned to go. "It only buys you time if you already know what you're doing."

He paused at the door. The hatch opened with a hiss.

"I never know what I'm doing," he said.

She grinned. "Exactly."

The mist outside thickened, swirling around him like static. Rook moved swiftly, just shy of running. The walls pulsed with faint light, revealing fractured reflections of the world above.

He didn't look back.

Rook had never thought of himself as political. Yet in the short time he'd served as head of security at Versailles Tower, he was learning that politics was the unseen battlefield. His father had always been one step ahead, a spy who tracked everyone at Elsinore Analytics with meticulous dossiers. Rook once dismissed it as paranoia, but now he saw it came from the war years, when survival meant reading people like maps and secrets were better than blades.

That same instinct was at work now, but Rook couldn't shake the feeling it was misdirected. Marr had ordered increased surveillance on Harrow—every optic feed tagged, every door log cross-checked, every conversation ghosted and filed. To Rook, it felt excessive. Harrow was reckless, sure, but not dangerous. Still, the reports stacked higher each day, and Rook found himself wondering if the scrutiny said more about his father's fears than about Harrow's crimes.

On Saturday he received a message from Pax, wrapped in heavy encryption. The words were spare, but the meaning cut deep: Harrow was moving against Viktor. How, Pax couldn't say—no plan, no timetable, just fragments and smoke. But the spark was real, the kind that didn't burn out once it caught. The fire was there, and Rook felt the heat even through the code.

He would have to decide. Harrow wasn't just a colleague—he was a friend, one of the few Rook trusted in a world that thrived on half-truths. But friendship had never been tested against loyalty this sharp. Viktor was his employer, his superior, the man who had elevated him into the glass-and-steel halls of Elsinore. Standing with Harrow meant betrayal. Standing with Viktor meant abandoning the one person who had never treated him as expendable. The choice wasn't abstract anymore; it was coming for him fast, and whichever way he leaned, the fallout would be permanent. For now, all he could do was carry it, heavy and unyielding, until the moment finally came.

CHAPTER 10

"Natural behavior must be rehearsed. Extemporaneous
authenticity cannot be trusted."

—Elsinore Surveillance Architecture Manual, Scene Composition v2.0

The conference room at Elsinore Analytics felt like a black hole filled with chairs. The narrow windows here were triple reinforced to survive bomb blasts and tinted to reduce the glare of neon from outside. Only faint, unnatural light emanated from recessed panels, sliding along the matte-black walls. The room was filled with the sharp smell of disinfectant and ozone—suggesting recent cleaning—clearing the room's memory. It was built during the war years, when dark rooms were standard, places without clocks or large windows, designed to smother both time and dissent. At the head of it all sat Viktor.

He sat perched in his chair like a predatory cat—sleek, elegant, and dangerous. His tailored suit shimmered with microscopic threads of reactive fiber, subtly shifting shades with his breathing, much like mood lighting designed to conceal and distract. His eyes, gleaming behind thin overlays of AR glass, tracked Keir with clinical detachment, assessing him as he moved.

Everyone wore the corporate look: polished shoes, sharp lapels, and hair styled to specifications. Bespoke suits, woven with soft, tactile fabrics, conveyed status through their design.

But beneath the polish, the tension showed.

Keir's fingers twitched at the cuff of his sleeve, futilely searching for a comforting biometric. His shoulders showed a slight, visible tightness typical of those who felt unprepared. He knew better than to fidget. This was Elsinore. Fidgeting could be flagged. It revealed weakness.

Viktor let the silence linger long enough to make him sweat, long enough to remind him who was really in charge of the room.

Beside Viktor, Corra leaned forward.

The soft glow from the interface panels cast delicate threads of light across her face, emphasizing the hollows under her eyes and the tension at the corners of her mouth. She appeared elegant, as always, but a closer look revealed the strain of maintaining that image—a stray hair or a strap of her dress slightly out of place.

"And?" she asked, voice steady, but threaded with tension. "What did you find?"

Keir paused long enough to let the silence speak.

"He admits to feeling … distracted," he said at last. Each syllable landed like a report he didn't want to file.

"And why?" Corra asked again, sharper now.

"He refuses to say."

"How convenient," she said.

Keir exhaled through his nose. "He dodges everything. Every question. The moment you think you've pinned him down, he's gone. It's almost like—"

"Madness?" Viktor finished, voice smooth but iron-cold.

Keir swallowed. "Methodical madness. Not incoherent. Detached. Calculated."

Viktor didn't move, but the temperature in the room dropped.

"Did he welcome you?"

Keir forced a smile. "Like a gentleman."

Everyone heard the equivocation.

"Polite," Keir said, recovering his poise. "Even friendly. But not present. Surface-level compliance. Like he wants to dodge the system."

Viktor leaned back. His lens overlays displayed translucent data across his eyes: probabilities, threat indexes, and decision trees.

"Did he show interest in anything?"

"The actors," Keir said.

Viktor's head tilted.

"I mentioned the troupe I hired," Keir said. "That caught him. He wants them brought in."

Viktor filed that away. A fixed point in a room full of variables.

"Entertain him," he said. "A distracted mind is a harmless one."

In the corner, Director Marr finally spoke. "He's already booked them," he said, with faint satisfaction. "There will be a performance Friday night."

Viktor didn't look at him.

Then he nodded.

"Good. Let's see if it changes anything."

Keir nodded. "Understood."

Viktor dismissed him with a flick of his fingers.

Keir left in silence. The door sealed behind him.

Corra didn't speak. But her hand curled against the chair, knuckles white.

Bjørn stepped forward, boots clicking against the polished floor. "Sir."

Viktor didn't look up right away. His eyes lingered on the holographic map hovering above his desk, the city outlined in arterial red, pockets of heat pulsing where the protests flared strongest. Only after a long pause did he tilt his head. "Any word on … what was her name?"

"Jessica Hvit," Bjørn said, voice clipped. "Yes. She has been neutralized."

Viktor's mouth curved—not quite a smile, more like a scar pulling taut. "Neutralized." He tasted the word as if testing it for quality. "And yet, they still rally in the streets. The dead are never as quiet as the living."

Bjørn shifted. "Apologies, sir. We're still … assessing leverage. Looking for ways to destabilize the protesters."

"Leverage." Viktor finally looked at him. The weight of his gaze was colder than the steel skyline beyond the glass. "You are not a man paid to look. You are a man paid to act. Do not confuse the two."

A silence stretched, thin as wire. Then Viktor flicked his fingers toward the door, dismissive. "Go. Make it stop."

Bjørn inclined his head, jaw tight, and turned on his heel. The echo of his footsteps lingered in the chamber long after he'd gone.

When the door slid shut, Viktor turned to Corra. Her face remained neutral, but her shoulders were tense.

"Corra," he said smoothly. "Leave us. Harrow is coming. We've arranged for him to be observed … in the company of Cassandra."

Her eyes flicked to his. "And if it is love?"

He gave a small smile. "Then perhaps her virtues will bring him back to himself."

Corra rose to exit with perfect grace, but as she passed Cassandra, she paused.

She placed a hand on the girl's shoulder—brief but charged with emotion.

"I hope you're right," she said. Her fingers lingered, a silent plea and a warning.

"I hope so too, madam," Cassandra said. But her eyes didn't meet her gaze.

Corra and the other executives had just left when Director Marr signaled for his daughter to approach the glass.

Outside, Elsinore City blinked in a tired simulation of vitality. Far below, protesters pressed against the cordons, their banners like fractured neon in the corporate glow. Their chants still carried the war's vocabulary—words of scarcity and survival, repurposed now for freedom. Cassandra's gaze lingered for a heartbeat longer than it should have. If she'd been free, she might have been down there with them, lost in the crush of voices.

Marr handed her a matte-black tablet, light as a feather, cold as steel.

"Read," he said. "Look distracted. The illusion of solitude sells the lie."

Cassandra obeyed.

She consistently obeyed. She'd done the math: obedient girls lasted longer.

Her serenity acted as a veil. Alone and unwatched—precisely how they needed her to appear.

Viktor lingered at the edge of her vision, not watching her but observing the space around her, searching for cracks in the staging that could break the illusion. He understood how to make lies pass for truth. It was a lesson refined during the Substrate War, when propaganda campaigns rewrote entire block histories overnight.

The room dimmed slightly.

A ping sounded—flat, unmistakable.

Movement alert. Upper corridor.

Harrow inbound.

Director Marr leaned in. "He's here. Move."

He and Viktor slipped behind a smart-glass partition. The iris closed completely. The lights dimmed. Their presence faded away.

They became part of the walls, unnoticed, always watching.

Cassandra stood alone in the chilly room, with the city behind her, the glass in front of her, and the performance beginning.

A woman alone. A woman apparently unwatched yet fully observed.

CHAPTER 11

"Love is not forbidden. Love is unscalable."

—HR Addendum: Noncompliance in Affectional Dynamics

Harrow entered the conference room for a meeting. The walls greeted him with silence—a tense quiet that somehow vibrated. Recessed lights faintly glowed overhead, offering no warmth. Neon from the skyline seeped through the smart-glass wall, casting a mosaic of blue and magenta across the polished black floor. The city stretched behind him, clinging to embers of power.

His steps were deliberate, measured, calibrated to prevent his shape from collapsing under the weight of what could not be spoken aloud.

He barely noticed Cassandra at first.

She remained still, near the far wall, illuminated from below by a tablet's glow. She didn't speak or move, a still-life inside a cathedral of surveillance. For a moment, she wasn't real.

Or maybe he wasn't.

To ghost the node, he thought, *drop the mask, sever the feed—or keep crawling between Earth and Heaven on scraped knees and malicious code.*

Death is a shutdown.

Fine!

But what if something's listening on the other side?

The soldiers of the war used to say the same—that even after the body fell, the system still logged the kill.

What if the audit runs deeper than the grave? What if the line stays open, even after the body's cold?

People die for less than I know. Live for worse.

Forget for comfort. Remember for pain.

So why am I still wired in?

Because fear is a better jailer than Marr ever was.

Because revenge feels like purpose, and purpose keeps the process alive.

Because if I cut the connection now, I lose the only thing that still sparks.

I won't flinch. Not yet. Not until the whole system crashes in a thunderous roar even the dead can hear.

Cassandra shifted in her chair.

The soft motion cracked the stillness like a dropped pin in a mausoleum.

She stood. Slowly. The floor beneath her registered no sound—built that way to mask human presence.

"Cassandra," Harrow said as he reached her.

She approached carefully, silhouetted by the shifting neon skyline through the glass behind her. Not a woman—a projection from some fragment of memory caught in the cache.

"Harry," she said, voice even. Formal as armor. "You've been dark for days. No pings, no trace. You okay?"

A dry smirk. A chuckle with no breath behind it.

"Appreciate the concern," Harrow said. "Really. I'm fine. Peachy. Rebooted three times just for the thrill."

She didn't answer. Instead, she lifted a parcel, precisely wrapped. Painful in its order.

"I've got your things," she said. "The old tokens—datachips, the synth-lily, that stupid analog letter you wrote on real paper. I've been holding them. Thought maybe you'd want them back."

Her hand didn't shake. But something behind her eyes did.

He stared at the package as if it were radioactive.

"Wasn't me," he said. "You're misremembering. Glitch in your cache."

Cassandra inhaled. Steady, but thin.

"Don't try to gaslight me, Harrow. You sent them. You wrapped your words in sugar-code, made them sparkle like the old sun. For a while, they meant something. But code degrades. Even pretty things rot when the soul behind them goes cold. Take them. They're corrupted now."

His eyes flickered with something that was not quite pain, not quite nostalgia. Something else.

Then he crossed the distance between them.

Too fast.

"Ha!" he said. "Are you honest?"

Cassandra blinked. "What?"

"Are you … *beautiful?*"

The words cracked the air.

"I don't follow," she said.

"If you're honest *and* beautiful, that's a design flaw. Shouldn't be linked. Purity and allure corrupt each other."

"Shouldn't beauty reflect virtue?"

"Hardly." His voice was clipped. "Beauty's just another virus. It rewrites you faster than morality can patch the breach. I've seen saints fall faster than malware hits a neural net."

She looked at him, defiant. Searching for the man she remembered.

He didn't meet her gaze.

"I thought I loved you once," he said.

She steadied herself. "You made me believe you did."

"You shouldn't have." His tone turned surgical. "I'm just skin over sin. Even when I try to be decent, the rot seeps through. No love. Just … latency."

It hit like shrapnel.

She didn't cry.

Not yet.

But her eyes shimmered—not with pain, but with clarity. She could see it now: not cruelty. Collapse. A man disintegrating in real time.

"Then I've been played," she said.

He stepped closer.

His voice dropped. Dangerous in its intimacy.

"Get out. Get safe. Cloister yourself, lock yourself in a tower, a convent—whatever keeps you from replicating the rest of us. I'm no better than the filth crawling these halls. I fantasize about blood, revenge, control. More sins than cycles to contain them. Why should scum like me get root access to the world? We're all broken code."

She froze.

A tear slipped down her cheek. Clean. Unflinching.

"Don't believe any of us," he said. "Especially not the ones who say they believe in you."

She held his gaze.

He looked away. It suddenly occurred to him that everybody was very late for this meeting.

"Where is your father?" he asked.

"In his office," she said too quickly.

His eyes widened.

He staggered back like a struck animal.

"Hope he's firewalled in," Harrow said. "Let him play puppet-master in his own sandbox."

His fists clenched.

"You want to marry? Fine. I'll drop you a wedding virus: no matter how clean your drive is, you'll still get blacklisted. Go cloister yourself. Or marry a fool. Someone too insignificant for the system to betray."

His voice rose, ragged.

"And don't think I don't see the paint you wear, the face God gave you overwritten with aftermarket lies. The sway, the coy sim routines, the baby-voiced seduction scripts. No more. I've had it. No more marriages. No more love. That's policy now."

He turned sharply.

"You want honesty? Fine. I'm done with confessionals and cover-ups. I've seen the numbers. And they don't add up."

His gaze cut across the room—past Cassandra, through the glass, to the wall where he knew the watchers waited.

He saw it now.

A single panel didn't quite reflect like the rest.

I see you.

Then he was gone.

He crashed through the room like a process terminating itself. The door susurrated open, and Harrow vanished down the corridor.

System termination complete.

Cassandra staggered back, legs giving way beneath her. She collapsed into the chair behind her, trembling.

The silence he left in his wake pulsed and throbbed.

The room appeared to close in on her. Lights were too bright. Glass was too clear. Walls were too smooth. She could sense the eyes behind them. Feel the recorders cataloging every breath.

Once, Harrow had been brilliance incarnate—a mind on fire, a voice that cracked like thunder and made people move. Now, he was something else.

A glitch disguised as a man. She loved him. Fiercely. Honestly.

And now, she sat with the unbearable weight of that love, now transformed into absence.

But even during the collapse, she understood what this was.

A test.

A performance.

The room wasn't empty. It was listening.

Director Marr and Viktor emerged from the shadows like villains in a mystery novel. Marr carried himself like he was back in the war councils—the same posture, carefully listening, calculating the best way to strike.

Neon from the city outside sliced across their faces in jagged streaks—blue and violet cutting through the dark like cold circuitry. They emerged not as men, but as reflections. Watchers. Architects of consequence.

Behind them, the surveillance console let out one final beep before going quiet. But the silence that remained wasn't clean. It buzzed with the echo of things overheard—grief stored, silence recorded.

Viktor exhaled sharply. The sound crackled in the air like static.

"Love?" he said, low and sharp, voice full of doubt. "That's not love. That's something else. Something broken. And whatever it is…" His fingers twitched at his side. "It's dangerous."

Director Marr didn't argue.

He stood with arms crossed, posture rigid. Always measuring. Somewhere between algorithm and paranoia.

"Perhaps," he said. "But love's in the equation. Twisted. Misrouted. Jammed into a place it doesn't belong—but present. That doesn't make it harmless. It just introduces a wildcard."

Viktor's jaw tensed. His gaze stayed fixed on the space Harrow had vacated, like he expected the floor to melt open.

"I'll send him to Neo-Paris," he said. "A shift in landscape. A quieter net. Distance between him and … all this."

There was no softness to it. Just control.

"New environment," he said, almost to himself. "New containment. Something to pull him out of the spiral before he erodes completely."

Director Marr was already building the framework.

He dragged a hand across his chin, eyes narrowed. "Sound strategy. But before he goes, let him speak to his mother. He still listens to her—underneath the static."

He flashed a smile that didn't reach his eyes.

"I'll position myself where I can listen."

Viktor turned toward him. His expression didn't change. He knew exactly what kind of man Marr was.

Then he nodded once. "Do it."

They stood in silence a moment longer.

Behind the smart-glass, Cassandra still sat in the chair. Her image blurred with reflections—the neon city, black glass, and the glint of tears. Her figure seemed small but not broken. The recording had ended, but the scene continued.

She was the afterimage.

The surveillance didn't blink.

The room hadn't emptied.

The watchers had simply started writing the next script.

Because they both understood a powerful truth:

The only thing more dangerous than madness … was the man who could file it, tag it, and make it useful.

CHAPTER 12

"Deviations from defined roles are classified as malfunctions
unless they can be successfully monetized."

—BEHAVIORAL COMPLIANCE LOG, PERSONALITY DRIFT CLAUSE 12

The lights were kept deliberately dim in Deck B7—no overhead
glare, only a cool glow from the floor runners and the tall vertical
displays that lined the wall like confessionals. The room was meant
for clarity, for observation without interference, but it felt like a
mausoleum in motion. Nothing but feed loops and filtered breath.
On one corner display, a muted exterior cam cycled past the protest
barricades several blocks away—flickers of banners, blurred mouths
chanting slogans that the system had stripped of sound. The camera
firmware still carried patches written durring the Substrate War,
back when silencing crowds was considered a military tactic, rather
than corporate protocol. Cassandra didn't linger on it, but Harrow
had noticed. She'd be out there if she could.

She stood at the central console, spine straight, posture neutral. Her silhouette was sharp against the monitor wall—a profile crafted for presence, not comfort. She wore a fitted blazer, dark gray with silver lapel accents. A simple line of code was inscribed just beneath the collar: *UNIT 3/STRATEGIC COMMS*. Harrow had seen her wear it a dozen times, but today it seemed more like armor than a uniform. The sleek braid pinned along the back of her skull was a statement, not a flourish. Functional. Elegant. Untouchable.

She didn't look up when the door sighed open for him.

"Five minutes late," she said, tone flat. Not reprimanding—just stating a fact.

Harrow stepped through the threshold, the door sealing itself behind him with a soft magnetic *thunk*. His coat hung unevenly over one shoulder, half-buttoned, as if he'd stopped caring about making anything symmetrical. A fresh scrape ran across the bridge of his knuckle, still faintly red beneath the skinseal. The scabbing hadn't fully set.

"I was recalibrating my moral compass," he said, tossing his access shard onto the side panel with a soft clatter. "Turns out it's defective. Factory defect, maybe."

Cassandra's fingers hesitated on the interface. Just for a moment. Then resumed.

"Funny," she said. "You used to keep it in near-perfect condition."

"Guess I let it slip." He came closer, boots clicking softly on the composite flooring. "You should see the rest of me."

"I have."

That landed sharper than either of them expected. Cassandra

didn't flinch. Just switched feeds on the display.

They watched the same looped footage from three angles: a mid-clearance security director returning home with a heavy briefcase, logging into an unlisted comms server, scrubbing trails. His name was Rael Vonn. His access keys were a little too flexible. His pulse rate spiked at unusual times. He was under quiet observation pending review.

It should've been a routine shadow report. Harrow was treating it like a prelude to war.

"You read the brief?" she asked, after a beat.

"Got the highlights." He leaned against the edge of the console, arms folded like a closed gate. "Rael's selling entry-layer biometrics to a third-tier shell. Used to be nervous about it. Now he's just methodical. Efficient. Doesn't even bother checking his six."

"You'd be surprised what people stop checking if they think no one's watching."

"I don't think you would," Harrow said. "You never stop watching."

That earned him a look.

"I mean that as a compliment," he added. "Mostly."

The room throbbed with soft ambient noise—barely perceptible subharmonics meant to regulate neural focus. Harrow hated it. It caused his thoughts to echo too vividly in his skull.

"I don't know what you're trying to prove," she said finally.

Harrow's mouth curled, bitter. "You think this is performance art?"

"I think it's erosion."

His hand hovered near the console's edge—like he was pondering whether to push the whole thing over.

"I'm not breaking," he said. "I'm evolving."

She turned to face him for the first time.

Up close, her expression was unreadable—yet not emotionless. Her eyes were too sharp for that, too focused. They darted over his face like scanning damage reports, assessing the drift. Her breath was controlled but shallow. She looked like someone who had practiced restraint so long it had become instinctive.

"You're not evolving," she said. "You're unraveling. And you want everyone around you to pretend it's progress."

Something flickered in Harrow's gaze. Not anger—he'd burned through that already. Just an old ache, flaring up like phantom pain in a limb he'd sworn he didn't miss. Soldiers from the Substrate War used to talk the same way—about wounds that never healed right, even when the flesh was replaced with alloy.

"Maybe I *am* unraveling," he said. "But at least I'm honest about it."

"Honest?" she shot back. "You've been lying to yourself and everybody else. What's worse: you're reckless about it."

Silence. Even the feed audio seemed to duck, ducking to let the aftermath breathe.

She stepped back, arms crossing tightly—bracing for something she didn't want to dodge again.

"Where are you going?" Harrow asked, softer now.

"To file the log."

"You're leaving because of me."

"I'm leaving because I don't know what you'll do next."

That stopped him cold.

"You used to," he said, quietly.

"I used to *think* I did."

Cassandra turned toward the door. It opened automatically, casting a narrow line of hallway light across the dark floor between them.

"You're not afraid of me," he said.

She paused, halfway out the door, one hand on the frame.

"I'm afraid of what you might become," she said.

Then she stepped outside. The door closed behind her.

Harrow didn't move.

The light from the surveillance wall flickered, casting pale gold lines across the floor—like prison bars, like data scars. He watched his own reflection in the dark glass of the console: blurred, fragmented, split across panes. Half of him flickered. The other half was gone.

He exhaled. Sharp. Measured. As if bracing himself to walk into a fire.

Maybe she was right. Maybe he *was* unraveling. But unraveling implied there was a thread to begin with—some coherent line that could be traced back to purpose.

He wasn't sure he'd ever had one.

He reached for the access shard and ran his thumb across the edge. It blinked once. Authentication ready. Mission parameters waiting. Another name, another mistake about to be logged into the system and called justice.

He pocketed it.

Across the room, the image of Rael Vonn looped again. Drinking. Typing. Pausing. Looking behind him.

It wasn't about Rael.

None of it ever was.

It was about the silence that followed—the crack no one acknowledged, but everyone tiptoed around. The part of you that quietly splintered in public—and the people who pretended not to see it because calling it out would make it real.

Cassandra had seen it. Still did. And now, she was leaving.

No. Not leaving. *Stepping back.*

That was worse.

He straightened his coat. Smoothed the collar. Turned off the console without logging the feed.

Another version of him might have sat with his feelings, traced them to their root cause, and written them out in code and regret. But that version was no longer there. What remained was leaner, colder—still himself, but pared down to duty. He had already chosen the role he would play.

CHAPTER 13

"Emotional instability is a resource. Instability can be directed, manipulated, and monetized."

—ELSINORE ANALYTICS: RISK-BEHAVIOR MODELING HANDBOOK

The subdeck was mostly empty at this hour—too low in the tower for executive traffic. A corridor built for function. A skeleton of pipes and cables webbed the ceiling, functional and unabashedly industrial. Much of it dated back to the Substrate War retrofit—utility veins rerouted overnight to keep the tower alive while the city starved below it. Every few meters, red hazard glyphs blinked in quiet pulses. No one came down here unless something was broken.

Somewhere far above, the protest lines would be forming for the night—faint vibrations of chants and bass-drum cadence carried down through the tower's frame. The rhythm was older than the protests themselves, inherited from the marches of the war years when people carried empty canisters like drums. You couldn't hear the words from here, but you could feel them in the metal, a low, persistent pulse under the hum of the pipes.

Pax followed the noise of work—clinks of metal, the faint sound of power tools, and the occasional muttered curse.

He found Harrow jammed halfway beneath an exposed vent assembly, illuminated by the dull glow of a freestanding diagnostic unit. His coat lay discarded, crumpled on the floor like a lifeless bird. His sleeves were rolled up to his elbows, exposing forearms marked with shallow scars and fading scan tattoos. His left hand gripped a stabilizer rod tightly. His right hand twisted a tool into the wiring with more aggression than finesse.

The air smelled of scorched metal and burned coolant. A machine about to fail.

"You're not assigned to this wing," Pax said.

Harrow didn't look up. "No one is. That's the appeal."

"This isn't on the system's repair log."

Harrow applied the final torque, then pulled his arm out with a grunt. "Doesn't mean it isn't broken."

He sat back on his heels and wiped his fingers on a strip of cloth, leaving faint smudges of machine grease on his palms. He appeared thinner than Pax remembered—sharp around the edges.

"Do I want to know what you're doing?" Pax asked.

"I'm recalibrating the airflow sensor."

"Why?"

"Because it's off by 0.03 degrees."

Pax crouched beside him, scanning the readout. "The system auto-corrects anything below 0.2."

"I wanted something to fix that doesn't tell me no."

Pax didn't say anything for a few seconds. He just watched him—measured his movements, the shallow rhythm of his breath, the tight way his jaw clicked whenever he spoke. Harrow wasn't twitchy. He was brittle.

"You've been avoiding the upper decks," Pax said.

"No," Harrow replied. "I've been avoiding people."

Pax's voice softened. "You mean her."

There was a pause.

Harrow picked up a different tool and spun it between his fingers like a coin. "Did she say something?"

"No," Pax said. "But she didn't have to."

A flicker crossed Harrow's face—barely perceptible but there. He took a quick breath and narrowed his eyes. He didn't like being read.

"She's upset," Pax said, "and not just in passing. This is different. She's moving like she's bracing for impact."

Harrow set the tool down carefully. "I didn't ask you to watch her."

"You didn't have to," Pax said. "You're not the only one who notices things."

"Fuck," Harrow muttered. "An observer with a moral compass."

"I'm not here to judge you," Pax said, calmly. "I'm here to figure out how long you think you can keep acting like this before something breaks."

"I'm not acting."

"No," Pax said. "You're spiraling."

Harrow suddenly stood up, brushing his hands on his pants. His posture was relaxed, but his shoulders were tense, screaming in contradiction.

"I have a plan," he said.

Pax raised an eyebrow. "Oh, good. Those always go well."

Harrow ignored him.

"During the play," he continued. "It's not just some performance. It's calculated."

Pax straightened. "You're staging something."

"I'm baiting a hook."

"For whom?"

"For Viktor."

Pax stared. "You're going to confront him *publicly*?"

"No. I'm going to *bait* him and see if he bites."

He approached the wall display, swiped to turn it on, and opened a script draft. Pax recognized it: the one Harrow had been refining with the internal comms team. What had started as a dry dramatization of the CEO's final moments had evolved into something stylized, personal, haunting.

Harrow scrolled to a line—one that read, "*The man who replaces a ghost wears his face like a stolen mask.*"

"See this?" he asked. "This is a cipher. A memory only Viktor and I would understand."

"You're embedding private references into the script?"

"References, no," Harrow said. "Fragments, intonations, allusions—nothing concrete, but enough to make him flash a tell. Enough to catch it on camera. Enough to confirm my suspicion."

Pax didn't look impressed. "You think he'll crack under stage lighting?"

"I think he'll react. A flicker. A twitch. The feed'll catch it."

"And that's your proof?"

Harrow's eyes darkened. "It's the beginning of proof. It's pressure. And pressure reveals cracks."

"And what if it doesn't?"

Harrow's voice lowered. "Then I escalate."

"To what?"

"I haven't written that part yet."

Pax rubbed the bridge of his nose. "Harrow, you're throwing yourself into your own trap."

Harrow stepped back. "I'm turning the system on itself. You know what they say about firewalls. Sometimes you only see what's behind them by breaching from within."

"And Cassandra?" Pax asked, carefully.

"She'll see the bigger picture when it works."

"You're assuming it *will* work."

Harrow's expression didn't waver. "She knows me."

Pax let the silence hang before answering.

"Knowing you," he said quietly, "isn't the same as trusting you."

Harrow said nothing.

"She's not afraid of your anger, Harrow," Pax added. "She's afraid of your direction—or the reckless lack of direction you're calling strategy."

"I'm not reckless," Harrow said. "I'm deliberate."

Pax nodded once. "Then *prove* it. Because if you go through with this, I'll have to be there—not because I like your plan, but because someone has to catch you when you fall."

That made Harrow glance at him—not softened, not grateful, but surprised, just for a second, as if he'd forgotten that anyone might care enough to stand by him.

Harrow looked away. The diagnostic screen behind him blinked once—*OPERATIONAL STABLE*. The vent was fine. There had never been a problem.

"I'm not trying to hurt her," he said.

"I know," Pax said. "But you are. And if this is the mission now—if you're willing to sacrifice everything for this single, shattering proof—then you better be ready to burn what's left if it works. And if it does... I'll help you shoulder what's left after the fire."

Harrow didn't reply. He moved to the corridor door and paused, one hand on the frame.

"Thanks for the check-in, Pax," he said. "Next time, bring cookies."

And then he left.

The door shut behind Harrow with its typical polished finality, as if sealing the conversation for the archive. Pax stood alone in the silence.

The faint mechanical hum of the diagnostics screen throbbed behind him like a second heartbeat.

He didn't move immediately. Just stood there, staring at the vent Harrow had been pretending to fix—clean paneling, fully operational. No fault to log. No damage to repair.

That was the part that got to him.

Harrow hadn't come here to fix anything. He'd come to feel like he was fixing something. To twist metal in his hands and calm the chaos in his head. Pax had seen that kind of behavior before—in soldiers, field agents, trauma patients who'd cycled through high-tier Elsinore mental conditioning.

Except Harrow had never broken. He didn't unravel. He *refined*.

Every time life cornered him, he came back sharper, meaner, and more focused.

And lonelier.

Pax exhaled through his nose. Then he slowly lowered himself onto the floor where Harrow had knelt, just to feel the room's temperature.

He leaned back against the wall panel, closed his eyes for a moment, and let the silence press in.

He remembered how Harrow used to move—before all this. Quick, yes, but not haunted. There was rhythm in him once. Momentum without blood. Now, everything was friction. Every gesture calculated. Every pause a blade half drawn.

He thought about what Harrow had said:

"*She knows me.*"

"*I'm not trying to hurt her.*"

But that was the thing.

Harrow never *tried* to hurt people. He simply refused to consider the consequences of his words and actions.

Pax ran a hand down his face, then glanced back at the diagnostic screen. The sensor data was steady. A perfect curve.

He tapped the console idly, bringing up the script Harrow had referenced. Line after line scrolled by—fragmented metaphors, weaponized nostalgia, phrases barbed with implications. Pax could see the shape of it now: a ghost story designed to bait. Not a tribute. A provocation.

It wasn't subtle. It was *personal*.

And it would work.

That was the worst part.

Pax sighed.

He wasn't afraid that Harrow's plan would fail. He was afraid it would succeed—and that the cost of proving Viktor's guilt would destroy Cassandra, destroy the little trust left between them, and turn Harrow into someone with no softness left.

And when it was over—when the ghost had been dragged into the light—there'd be nothing left.

Pax shut the console down. He hesitated, then slipped the script file onto his own device—to carry a copy. A way to be ready. A way to share the weight when it all came down.

He stood slowly, took one last look at the empty corridor beyond the door, then turned off the lights.

CHAPTER 14

"No system is truly secure."

—Internal Risk Memo, Elsinore Analytics Red Team Dossier

The sky above Neo-Paris pulsed with gray static layered with red bleed. Rook crouched inside the skeletal frame of an old repeater shell, four stories above the street, in a part of town where drones don't bother to scan. The shell itself was a war relic, one of thousands installed during the Substrate War to keep the networks alive when the grid fractured. The wind up here had teeth. It gnawed at his coat, pulled at the edges of his collar, consuming his warmth particle by particle.

He didn't mind. Cold reminded him that he was alive.

The disc in his hand had warmed slightly. Matte black when he left Kira's, it now pulsed a faint cyan at the edge—active, but not engaged. Rook didn't fully trust it. It was too small, too simple. A sleek circle with no label, no backup, no visible tech. It looked like a trinket someone would wear around their neck.

And yet, it was the only thing that would allow him to contact someone inside Elsinore without setting off every optic and audit filter in Viktor's office.

He crouched lower, bracing himself with one hand while he opened a corroded signal panel with the other. The repeater's shell was rusted through, but the relay port still blinked as he bypassed the voltage buffer. Good enough. He pulled a line from his coat—shielded, short-range, gold-tipped—and inserted the disc into the junction.

The air changed.

The hum of ambient surveillance faded away. A deep, steady pressure filled his ears, like the world had gone underwater. He'd heard veterans describe that same pressure in the war, when blackout jammers silenced whole districts. The city lights dimmed slightly around him—bowing to the signal's demand for silence.

A short chirp. Connection routed. Encrypted node-to-node. No tower ID.

Line active. Two minutes.

He keyed the name.

PAX // INTERNAL OPS

It rang once.

"I hope you're somewhere I won't have to explain," Pax said, voice sharp and alert.

"I could say the same to you," Rook replied. His voice was calm, but his fingers flexing against the relay told a different story.

"How the fuck did you—never mind. What is this, a ghost call?

You're bouncing through junk satellites."

"Paid for two minutes of silence."

"That disc better be from someone I trust."

"You don't trust anyone."

"Exactly."

A pause. Then Pax again, quieter: "What's wrong?"

Rook leaned forward, shoulder brushing steel. "Viktor's watching Harrow."

"Viktor watches everyone."

"No. I mean *watching*-watching. Direct feed. Personal deck. Full attention."

The sound of Pax exhaling crackled softly. "Yeah. I know. I've seen it."

"How bad is it?"

"He's running simulations. Dual prediction models. One says Harrow's going to spiral into a full-blown public meltdown. The other says he's playing harmless while lining up a quiet takeover."

"And Viktor believes both?"

"He doesn't know what to believe. That's what makes him dangerous."

Rook clenched his jaw. "What about Cassandra?"

"He's started watching her, too."

Rook didn't speak. Didn't move.

"Because Harrow broke it off," Pax said. "Three days ago. No warning. Just—cut the cord."

"He what?"

"Walked out on her like she was a glitch in his sequence."

Rook closed his eyes briefly. "That doesn't make sense. I mean, I told her he would, but I didn't think he'd actually do it."

"Nothing he's doing makes sense anymore. Not on the surface." Pax sounded tired now, not just physically but soul-deep without optimism. "Cassandra barely leaves her flat anymore. Lab's dead. Systems running loops. She left her door open yesterday."

"She still have the files?"

"She hasn't purged them. But she's not touching them either. I think she's waiting for a reason."

"Or trying to forget she ever had one," Rook muttered.

The wind stirred around him, caught on the antenna ribs, and made them hum softly. He checked the disc—seventy-four seconds remaining. Time always seemed to move faster when the world was bleeding out beneath you.

Pax asked, "You coming back?"

"Not yet."

"Why not?"

"Because it's not time."

"He needs help."

"He doesn't want help."

"So what—you're just going to orbit the mess? Watch it collapse from a safe distance?"

Rook's voice was quieter than Pax expected. "No one's safe, Pax. That's the point."

"Then why this? Why the disc, the ghost signal, the off-grid reach-out?"

"I needed to know if he was burning alone," Rook said. "Or if he was going to take everyone with him."

"The protests are picking up," Pax said. "People demanding bodily autonomy."

Same fault line the war had opened—despair over substrate, control of who lived and how long. Only the slogans had changed.

"How about accountability?"

"They'll get there."

Rook sighed.

The wind screamed. The lights below shimmered. Far across the cityscape, a flare streaked through the sky—blue flame, followed by the hum of a patrol cruiser passing close by.

The disc chirped twice—final warning.

Pax's voice came fast. "If you're going to move, Rook, *move soon*. He's not going to hold himself together for much longer."

Rook stood slowly. "That's the plan."

"And if he dies trying to do this alone?"

Rook looked out over the city. "Then I make sure someone remembers what he tried to do."

The line cracked.

"Rook—"

The disc blinked once before shutting down silently. No heat, no trace. The fiber port it occupied flickered and went dark, as if it had dreamed the entire exchange.

Rook stood there, coat flaring in the rooftop wind, eyes scanning the fractured skyline. He reached into his inner coat pocket, felt the jagged disc's weight, and closed his fingers around it. He slid it back into place. Some things could wait. For now, the silence held him.

CHAPTER 15

"The illusion of stability is preferred. Consistent emotional
suppression will project strength."

—EMOTIONAL PERFORMANCE HANDBOOK, COMPLIANCE PSYCHOLOGY V5.1

By Friday evening, Cassandra hadn't slept.

She'd lain in the dark with her optic filters dimmed, her heart ticking against the quiet like a warning she couldn't ignore. Somewhere below her—the 44th floor, she thought—someone was adjusting the lighting for a gala. Always a gala. Her ceiling flickered faintly with the bleed, soft bursts of gold washing over artificial plaster.

She stared into it as if daring it to blink first.

A system reminder crackled through the speaker: "One hour until curtain."

She hadn't agreed to go to the play. But she hadn't said no either. That's how it worked here. Refusal caused a red flag on a behavioral log. Silence was always consent.

She sat up. Crossed to the vanity.

Her reflection was symmetrical. Untouched. Nothing out of place.

She opened the narrow drawer beneath the vanity, fingers finding the smooth edge of the Saint Mary coin her mother had given her. A quick brush with her thumb, then she set it back in its place. A silent benediction, unrecorded, before she faced the cameras.

"Run diagnostics," she whispered, and her lenses obeyed. Pupil response normal. Pulse within range. No signs of intoxicants or hormonal irregularity.

Emotion: Indeterminate.

Recommended intervention: none.

She almost laughed. *None.*

They'd tagged her as emotionally stable. She'd seen the notation. *Emotionally stable. Composed under pressure. Perfect for contrast.* Marr had praised her for it once, years ago, when she'd walked out of her mother's funeral without smudging her eyeliner.

He'd meant it as a compliment.

She had been twelve years old.

He'd learned to value that kind of composure in the Substrate War, when grieving too loudly could get you noticed—and noticed meant erased.

Her movements were precise, almost machine-like. Black slacks, tailored for a perfect balance between allure and understatement. A silk blouse—just enough softness to seem human. She wore just enough makeup to be appropriate for the occasion. She didn't need to stand out—or to be questioned.

Everything she wore communicated one message: stable. Controlled. Harmless. She paused in the hallway. Her suite's surveillance node blinked red.

Always watching. Now more than ever.

She leaned in close enough to fog the sensor and whispered, "How do I look?"

No response, of course. Just a gentle mechanical whirr as the lens focused.

Cassandra sidestepped the busy green room, avoiding the groups gathered near the stage. Their laughter and chatter echoed in her ears. Too many voices. Instead, she quietly moved through the dimly lit corridor behind the stage, where flickering lights cast eerie shadows. Finally, she stepped onto the east maintenance platform, a secluded space that offered a sweeping view of the river below. The water meandered lazily, its surface dull gray, glittering with discarded debris that looked like forgotten treasures. Far below the tower, beyond the cordoned perimeter, protest lines pressed against the barricades, their banners a fractured ripple of color in the corporate gloom. They marched with the same cadence their parents used during the war, the rhythm of ration queues and blackout vigils reborn as protest. She couldn't hear the chants from this height, but she could imagine them — steady, stubborn, refusing to fade.

As she leaned against the cool glass railing with her palms flat on the surface, the reflection staring back at her wavered and distorted, blurring her features so they mirrored her turbulent thoughts.

Two months ago, she'd been caught in a burn-hot romance. Two weeks ago, she had half-convinced herself Harrow was going to propose—seen it in the way his gaze lingered, the pauses that seemed to gather courage. Two days ago, she still believed she could pull him clear of the wreckage, steer him past the grief that clung to him like a second skin. But now … now she feared that grief had calcified into something cold, heavy—a stone, pulling what remained of his humanity down into black water where light could never touch it again. When he spoke, there were ghosts in his voice—quiet, restless things that made her afraid she was already too late.

She tapped her wrist, and the rewritten, realigned digital script of *The Murder of Claudius* appeared. She scanned the margins: bolded cues, time-coded gestures. A line had been added: "He pushes his brother from the roof."

She knew that line. It wasn't from the archive. Harrow had added it. Of course he had.

She tried to imagine Viktor watching the scene. Did he realize what Harrow had done? Did he care? Would he flinch, or would he smile as he always did, as if nothing in the world could affect him behind his layer of biometric armor?

A chime rang on her implant.

It was Marr's voice: "Do not improvise. Do not deviate. Be precise."

She shut it down.

She was finished being a control variable.

Let them run their experiment. Let them measure her posture, her tears, and her pupil dilation during Act III. She would play her part with precision—a performance entirely her own.

CHAPTER 16

"A compelling lie will effectively mask an inconvenient truth."

—Narrative Engineering Memo, Messaging Department v9.1

The performance hall at Elsinore Analytics stood as a monument to corporate spectacle, designed to impress. Its architecture embodied pure brutalism—every sinew of the building laid bare: steel beams resembling tendons, ductwork like veins, plumbing and power conduits running in orderly bundles beneath a skin of onyx-black paint. It was a space that seemed to invite inspection, as though nothing here was hidden—yet every surface bristled with embedded sensors, silently cataloging the tilt of a head, the shift of a stance, microexpressions flickering across faces. The air carried a faint scent of ozone and machine oil, the smell of a place powered by voltage rather than breath. A soft electrical hum vibrated through the hall's bones, almost subliminal, like the purr of a patient predator. Above, neon tracers streaked across the ceiling in programmable constellations, their shifting hues tuned to the AI's reading of the performance's emotional tone. The lights never rested. The system never blinked.

At the heart of everything was the stage—a floating, circular platform surrounded by concentric rings of haptic seating—that resembled an altar. The floor was a seamless pane of reactive glass, faintly glowing with embedded circuitry, synchronized live with the actors' movements. Every gesture, expression, and pause was tracked, enhanced, and refined. The actors, dressed in smart-fabric that changed color and opacity in real time, appeared more like myth than men. Their faces were overlaid with digital projections—masks coded by Harrow himself.

Above them, separated by an invisible barrier of security measures and self-delusion, was the executive suite, suspended like a predator's perch above the theater. Its tinted smart-glass windows looked down on the spectacle below with chilling detachment. Viktor lounged at the center of the VIP gallery, a goblet of synthwine in one hand, eyes half-lidded. But he was watching. Always watching. Beside him, Corra's expression flickered between forced engagement and unease. Director Marr leaned forward slightly, his augmented lenses adjusting automatically to capture and tag each performance beat for later analysis.

The rest of the suite was peppered with expressionless elite operatives, dressed in black suits. Department heads. Strategy officers. Surveillance directors. All pretending to be there for love of the art.

But Harrow knew better.

He stood alone in the shadows behind the stage, watching the final calibration run through the system's HUD. He'd touched every file, adjusted every cue, and modified the emotional register of the lead actor's voiceprint. He also rewired the pacing algorithms to exaggerate pauses in a specific scene. Subtle. Precise. Devastating.

This wasn't merely theater.

It was a scalpel to the soft tissue of Viktor's guilt.

The rewritten lines weren't merely provocative—they were direct accusations hidden in metaphor and myth. Harrow had dismantled the traditional play and reconstructed it as a digital mirror: a ghost story disguised as entertainment. A murder dressed as a performance. He had given the stage director strict override commands. The murder scene would linger. The actors would glance too long at the gallery glass.

And Viktor would see himself.

If he flinched, if he reacted—Harrow would know. The mask would crack. The lie would unravel. That was the plan.

But the plan was also a noose, and Harrow was already tightening the rope around his own neck.

He wasn't entirely sure what he'd do if it worked.

Or what he'd do if it didn't.

The fictional CEO stood at center stage, wind tearing through his smart-fabric coat as the rooftop scene played out in flickering neon rain. The illusion of weather shimmered around him, hyperreal and eerily cinematic, projected in high-res particle light against the backdrop of a fractured skyline.

He turned. Faced his brother.

The rooftop set stretched across the stage like a digital cliff's edge. Light pulsed along its seams—warnings built into the design.

The actors didn't move like typical performers. The AI's performance algorithms tracked them to human movements, learning from hours of surveillance footage. he base code came from war simulations—training AIs that had once studied soldiers in trench alleys and riot lines, now recycled to teach actors how to die convincingly. The CEO's fingers twitched slightly before the blow landed, a data-driven imitation of instinct. The brother's shove seemed like hesitation, then a decision.

A death reenacted.

The CEO fell.

The platform below caught him in complete silence—then activated the crash-response soundscape: a wet impact, deep and final. A shriek followed, perfectly timed. The wife's scream, enhanced by directional acoustics, pierced through the hall with the raw clarity of grief. It was grief in high definition—engineered, exaggerated, unbearable.

And then came the pivot.

She turned to her brother, her hand reaching out for his.

It was effortless, practiced.

The transfer of power happens not through signatures or succession plans but through gestures and touch.

Above, behind the soundproof glass, Viktor shifted.

His fingers twitched on the armrest of his chair—once, twice—then held firm in a grip just shy of white-knuckle tension. The chrome edge of his cybernetic eye flashed red and gold. He didn't blink. But the muscle in his jaw tensed hard enough to peg the biometric scanner.

The system *was* reading him. Harrow made sure of it.

From the shadows of the executive gallery, Harrow leaned toward Pax, his voice low, steady, unblinking. "He's getting nervous."

Pax didn't respond. He didn't need to.

Viktor's eye flashed again—just a glitch. But it lingered. Subroutine failure crept across the lens like tiny cracks. Panic ricocheted through him in quick bursts, too fast to hide.

Below, the usurper on stage claimed the crown.

Viktor's hand moved.

The glass tipped over. Ice struck the table, sharp as gunfire broke the silence. Liquor spilled in a fan of digital shards across the dark tablecloth, like corrupted data spreading across a compromised system.

The gallery froze.

Board members turned, one by one. Executives half-rose. Even Corra's posture stiffened.

Viktor's illusion cracked.

"*Lights,*" he said, voice amplified by internal comms. The word was a failsafe trigger. Emergency override engaged.

The holograms flickered. The AI faltered, caught in the sudden shutdown command. Characters on stage wobbled. Their digital faces fractured and disappeared. The rooftop dissolved into white noise. The actors stood blinking and limp, like puppets whose strings had been cut.

Viktor stood now.

Not a CEO. Not a husband.

A man with a detonator in his hand and sweat at his collar.

"*Shut it down*," he said, voice brittle beneath the steel. There was no velvet now. Just raw wire.

Harrow stood still in the corner.

He watched.

He knew what fear looked like.

He'd been raised in its shadow.

And now, it was Viktor's turn.

Director Marr fumbled with his earpiece and barked garbled commands into the system as the performance disintegrated into glitch and confusion. One of the actors staggered, their smart-fabric costume dissolving into static, with their face flickering between identities before vanishing. Another frozen midline, trapped in a system loop until someone manually severed the feed.

The audience swarmed—executives blinked out of their trance and scattered, whispers erupted like firewall breach alarms. A cleanup protocol was activated overhead, and drones descended to contain the chaos. But the damage had already been done.

Corra followed Viktor's exit, her heels whispering softly on the alloy floor. She didn't speak, but her gaze lingered on the stage as she passed. Her expression wasn't grief. It wasn't even confusion. It was calculation—measuring the weight of what had just been broken open and what she might need to do to survive it.

Harrow stretched his arms, savoring a moment of personal vendetta. He looked up toward the dark glass that once reflected power. "The guilty flee fastest when spooked," he said with a grin. The server drone hovering beside him paused, waiting for input.

Pax stood nearby, arms crossed, still scanning the logs. "You were right," he said. "His reaction breached all protocol."

Harrow's smile unfolded like a blade. "The ghost was right," he said. "The play was the thing."

He turned to the server drone, its chrome body reflecting twin images of himself on its mirrored surface. "Bring me a drink," he said. "And music. Something with strings. I'm in a mood."

The drone blinked once and disappeared.

Keir approached. His body language was neutral to the point of parody, but his eyes betrayed him—half-embarrassed, half-afraid.

"Harrow, sir," Keir began. Diplomatic. Dry as recycled air. "Viktor requests your presence."

Harrow took the drink from the returning drone and took a slow, deliberate sip. "Drunk, is he?"

"No, sir," said Keir, stiff. "Angry."

Harrow tilted his head. "For a moment, I feared he'd grown a conscience."

"Your mother," Keir said, "also wishes to see you. Immediately."

"A mother's concern," Harrow said, placing a hand over his heart in mock sincerity. "Touching."

"Your actions disturb her," Keir said, jaw tight.

"Oh, wonderful son," Harrow said, "to astonish his mother!"

He set the drink down. His eyes flicked toward the idle musicians still loitering near the stage. "Before I go, something … orchestral."

Keir took a step forward. "Harrow—"

Harrow raised a single finger. The room froze.

He grabbed a recorder from the table, flipped it over as if testing the weight of a blade. It was a child's instrument—harmless in appearance but weaponized in his hand.

"Play something for me," he said.

Keir hesitated. "I don't know how."

Harrow smiled. "It's simple. Cover the holes, blow some air, make sound."

"I don't know how," Keir said again, softer now.

The smile stayed, but something behind his eyes snapped shut.

"How curious," he said, stepping closer. "You don't know how to make music, Keir. But you think you can tune me? Press the right sequence and hear your master's voice come through?"

Keir stood perfectly still.

"You think you can press my stops," Harrow said, "run your fingers along the right scripts, and make me sing for him?"

He dropped the recorder onto the table. The sound echoed, hollow and final.

"Tell my mother I'll come," he said. "Soon."

Director Marr entered then, tension pinched at his brow.

"Harrow," he said, trying for calm. "Corra is waiting."

Harrow didn't move. He pointed lazily toward the darkened skyline beyond the glass.

"Do you see that cloud?"

Marr blinked. "Which one, sir?"

"That one. Looks like a dragon, doesn't it?"

"I ... suppose it does."

"No, wait. A fox."

A pause.

"Yes. Perhaps."

"Or a wolf."

"Very much like a wolf," Marr said, now clearly off-balance.

Harrow smiled faintly.

"That's the thing about 'soon,' Director Marr," he said. "It means whatever the fuck I want it to mean."

"Sir," Marr pressed, his voice sounding strained. "This can't wait."

Harrow turned, adjusted his collar, and nodded once. "Fine. I'm coming."

Director Marr exhaled and left.

As the door closed, Pax stepped closer.

"What now?"

Harrow rolled his shoulders like a fighter loosening up before the bell. "Midnight approaches," he said.

Pax didn't smile. Harrow's victories always came with fallout. "And when the demons come?" he asked.

Harrow's eyes flashed with something cold. "They play," he said.

He walked forward, into the corridor, into the dark.

The night wasn't over.

It was only beginning.

CHAPTER 17

Viktor paced the length of his penthouse sanctuary, a glass-and-steel cathedral overlooking Elsinore's sprawling skyline. The city pulsed beneath him, a web of neon veins running through the sky—bright, sprawling, impossible to escape. Beyond the floor-to-ceiling windows, drones darted through the night, data streams flickered between towering industrial monoliths. The empire beneath his feet was his to command. Yet, control was slipping from his grasp.

The room was pristine. The vaulted ceiling resembled old-world cathedrals, complete with chrome-ribbed arches glowing with artificial starlight. Black marbled floors mirrored the projected star field.

Viktor's AuRORA pulsed against his temples, feeding him

silent updates: stock fluctuations, protest node chatter, flickering sentiment spikes. He dismissed them with a twitch of his eyes. But the unease persisted. The play had done more than provoke. Harrow hadn't simply accused him. He'd exposed him. Made him feel regret. Made him feel trapped.

He paused before a prayer alcove—a ceremonial display, designed for appearances. The AI there presented a menu of spiritual subroutines: Judeo-Christian, Zen, and stored pagan fragments. It flickered on, casting synthetic light across his face. For a moment, he appeared almost saintly.

He knelt. Burdened but not reverent.

"My offense is rank," he said aloud, voice cutting the hush. The machine returned nothing. He stared into the haloed glow, but there was no absolution. Only code. And he felt the weight now.

Beyond the killing, the resonance lingered. The corruption that followed was inevitable. He'd done more than erase a man; he'd rewritten the future in blood.

Harrow saw it.

Harrow knew.

Viktor squeezed his eyes shut. His breath hitched. His hands clenched—not in prayer, but in something close to grief.

He wanted to pray. To repent.

He wanted to mean it.

But there was no repentance without surrender.

And he would surrender nothing.

Not power. Not the crown. Not her.

He rose slowly, smoothing his suit. The moment vanished behind him like a door quietly closing.

Heaven would not forgive him, but hell would have to wait.

Harrow was a threat now. A liability. A variable.

He would send him to Neo-Paris.

Immediately.

And make sure he did not come back.

Outside, the city pulsed—unconcerned, impossibly vast. A kingdom built on secrets and silence.

And Viktor let himself believe that stillness could stand in for absolution.

Harrow lingered in the corridor outside the sanctum, the hush pressing against him like a sealed vault. The walls here absorbed sound, every breath rebounding against silence until it felt consecrated, inviolate. His optics shifted focus, narrowing until the glass partition dissolved into clarity.

He saw inside, Viktor bowed before the altar's sterile glow. The light haloed him, erasing the lines of his face until he looked less like a man than a projection of power rehearsing contrition. Lips moved in measured rhythm, too polished to be prayer.

A perfect chance.

Harrow's hand ghosted beneath his coat. His fingers found the dagger's hilt—alloy wrapped in polymer, cool as stone. The blade hummed awake at his touch, a low vibration eager for release. One motion, one severed spine, and everything would be finished. No trial. No defense. Only blood on the marble and silent judgement where a tyrant had knelt.

The weapon throbbed, hungry.

But Viktor was praying.

Harrow's grip whitened. His pulse hammered in his ears, the cadence of old war-drums. It was the same rhythm broadcast across his childhood, the static lullaby of a generation raised beneath sirens and propaganda. His father's voice echoed with it—begging for release, dying without rites, without absolution. Condemned to silence.

And now this usurper dared to kneel as though salvation could be staged. Dared to mouth words of repentance before a machine that recorded everything and forgave nothing.

To strike him here would be to grant him a mercy his father never had. It would make Viktor a penitent king, ushered into death with counterfeit grace. That was no justice. That was release.

Justice demanded spectacle. Exposure. Harrow wanted the city to see Viktor stripped bare, to see the blood he spilled clotting on his hands, to watch him fall not as a martyr but as a fraud. When the blade descended, it would not cut through prayer. It would cut through arrogance, through sin, through the certainty that power made him untouchable.

Slowly, deliberately, Harrow released the hilt. The blade dimmed, its glow retreating like a system going dark.

Not tonight. Not in prayer.

When Viktor died, it would be in disgrace. And Harrow would make sure the world bore witness.

He stepped back into the corridor's shadows, every movement measured, a patient ghost returning to his vigil. His mother still lived. His chance would come.

And when it did, the record would be complete—unaltered, undeniable, eternal.

CHAPTER 18

"When containment fails, sanitize the evidence."

—SECURITY RESPONSE PROTOCOL, TERMINATION DIRECTIVE V4.2

The lights were dim—a red-gold sunset streaming through tinted smart-glass. Corra stood alone. The room reeked of legacy and cover-ups—its fine veneer hiding the corruption and deceit that permeated the tower.

Marr's voice buzzed through her skull, patch-routed on a private node even though he stood behind one of her curtains. "He's *en route*. Hit him hard. Tell him the chaos he's left in his wake is no longer containable. Let him know you've burned favors shielding him, and that's done. I'll be silent. Just deliver the message."

She severed the connection with a twitch of her eye. Footsteps echoed from the corridor—a smooth, predator's pace.

Then he was there.

"What's the emergency, Mother?"

Corra straightened her posture, the crisp fabric of her cuffs snapping into place like pieces of armor ready for battle. She said, flat with contempt, "You've brought shame upon your father."

Harrow's lips curled into a sardonic smile, a flicker of defiance in his eyes. "You chose to marry the man who was responsible for my father's death. Seems we're both in the same boat, don't you think?"

"That's absurd," she snapped, fists curling at her sides.

"No, that's you projecting your guilt onto me," Harrow replied, his voice cool as ice.

"What in the world are you even talking about, Harrow?" She frowned, confused.

"What's the matter, Mother? Is there a glitch in your memory feed?" Harrow's sarcasm cut through the air, sharp and biting.

With a glacial stare, Corra pressed on: "Have you forgotten who I am?"

"Not a chance," Harrow said, smiling without warmth. "You're the Chief Financial Overseer of this gilded sarcophagus. Wife to a backstabbing corporate parasite. And … my mother."

"Then I'll call someone who'll make you listen." She moved toward the wall panel.

Harrow blocked her way, standing imposing and unyielding. "Don't," he said. His voice was low. Calm. He stepped closer, invading her personal space, making her acutely aware of the tension thrumming around them.

"You're not leaving this room until you confront the truth of what you've become. Until I rip off the mask and show what's underneath." His eyes bore into hers, dark and unwavering.

"Would you truly hurt me? Is that what you intend?" Her voice broke. "Security!" she cried, but the word fell flat—like static in a dead channel.

Something shifted behind the drapes. Small. Close.

"Emergency protocol, now!" called a muffled voice, distant yet urgent—a flicker of hope rising and falling like a tide.

But it was too late.

With a swift, fluid motion, Harrow unsheathed his dagger. The blade caught the light. Bright and cold. "A rat in the walls? Let's clean house," he murmured, almost savoring the thought.

In an instant, he lunged at the shadowy presence, and the body crumpled to the ground, lifeless, warm blood steaming against the cold composite floor.

"God … damn …" a stunned whisper escaped his lips as he recoiled slightly, the weight of the act washing over him.

Corra's scream cut through the stillness. "What the hell have you done?"

Harrow knelt to check the corpse. He yanked the curtain aside. Marr stared up with dead eyes. Still twitching. Already forgotten. "Wrong target. Thought it was the CEO. Turns out it was his mouthpiece." He looked down at Marr. "Should've stayed in the shadows, old man."

Harrow turned to Cora. "Stop with the theatrics. Sit. Now. Or I'll sit you down myself."

Corra trembled. "How dare you—"

"Dare? You wanna talk about what you dared, Mother? You turned love into stock options. You made virtue a mask for survival instinct. And you married a man who killed my father and had a corporate obituary written before the body cooled."

He snapped his fingers. AR projections flared to life—portraits: his father and Viktor, side by side. One dignified, radiant. The other bloated with power and corruption.

"You left this—for that? You call that logic?"

"Harrow, please. Stop—"

"Still letting him touch you?" Harrow asked. "Still letting him sweat on you in that polished dungeon you call a bed? That's not love. That's submission."

"You're twisting everything I say into a weapon," Corra whispered.

"Good. Because I'm out of patience and out of hope."

"You've gone mad."

A chill spread through the room. The shadows lengthened—wrong, alive. Then, with an almost imperceptible shift in the air, a presence materialized—an unsettling sensation like static that brushed against the teeth, stirring a deeply primal instinct. The ghostly figure appeared. A flicker of Silas Eisler—ghost, glitch, something in between. It was as if his essence were caught between the digital and the physical world, a fragment that could never find peace.

"Father …"

Corra instinctively recoiled, her heart racing. "No. No—he's hallucinating," she muttered under her breath, desperation bleeding into her tone.

"Did I fail you?" Harrow asked, his voice a painful blend of hope and despair. "Am I too slow, too soft? Tell me."

The phantom's gaze was unwavering. "No," he said. "You're drifting. I came to realign the mission. She's breaking. Speak to her. Save what's left."

Harrow stood still, turning his body toward Corra with a furrowed brow. "Can't you see him? No? That tracks; you only see what benefits you," he said, his words laced with frustration.

"There's nothing there," Corra pleaded, her voice teetering on the brink of panic. "Nothing! You're chasing phantoms, shadows of what you wish were real."

"Then why does he look at me like that?" Harrow pressed, anguish creeping into his voice. "Why do his eyes still demand justice?"

The ghost, heavy with the weight of unresolved grief and longing, faded into the air, its form dissipating like morning mist, leaving only a faint chill.

"It's in your mind."

"No, Mother, you're blocking it. You won't face it. You'd rather blame me. But it's not going away."

"You've broken my heart," she said with a sob.

"Then throw away the corrupted half."

He gestured to Marr's body. "Didn't mean to kill him. But maybe it had to be done."

"What should I do?" Corra asked.

Harrow considered this a moment and then said, "Don't tell Viktor I'm sane. Let him think I've cracked. Let him make mistakes."

"I won't speak a word," Corra said, as if making a vow.

"I'm bound for Neo-Paris. Did you know?"

"I… forgot. They've arranged it."

"Sealed packets," Harrow said coolly. "My old schoolmate—Keir, a corporate errand boy—is the delivery drone. They think I won't see it coming. But I've got a payload waiting for them. It'll be poetic. Two birds. One blast radius."

He nodded to Marr's corpse. "This mess? It'll simply hurry things along. I'll dispose of him. You—try not to become a villain in this tale."

He dragged the body toward the corridor, getting blood on his hands. Over his shoulder, he called out, "Good night, Mother. Don't choke on what's left of your conscience."

CHAPTER 19

"If a subject can no longer be controlled, reclassify. If
reclassification fails, erase."

—Executive Risk Index Protocol, Identity Stability Clause 5.3

Harrow washed the blood from his hands. The corridor around him
flickered with dim blue emergency lights, its steady thrum contrast-
ing with the heavy silence. The air smelled strongly of ozone. Behind
him, shadows still carried the burnt scent of circuits and ionized
blood. The body—Director Marr—was gone. Disassembled. Vapor-
ized. Wiped from the server. This kind of erasure was perfected in
the Substrate War—when soldiers didn't just die, they were scrubbed
from rosters, identities overwritten until even grief had nothing to
hold on to.

And now …

Footsteps—more than one set—echoed quickly and sharply off
the polished alloy floor, like accusations made physical.

"Where's the body, Harrow?" Keir's voice rang out, trying to hold an air of authority where it no longer existed.

Harrow didn't turn. He kept his gaze fixed on the wall ahead—one of Elsinore's many reflective surfaces, each image glitching at slightly different speeds. He tilted his head.

"Archived," he said. "Returned to the base code."

"We need to retrieve it. The board wants it handled discreetly. The chapel—"

"The chapel? That data-vault with candles? That's not prayer, that's formatting."

"Please, Harrow, I have to—"

"Do you?" Harrow's voice cut through the air like static. He turned slowly, his eyes unreadable behind the flickering glow of his optics. "And I—I need to believe you're more than a data-mining bot in a bespoke suit. What response is a CEO's son supposed to give to an interrogation algorithm that once knew how to laugh?"

Keir blinked. "What are you talking about?"

Harrow smiled bitterly. "You, dear Keir, are a sponge."

"A … sponge?" The word sat awkwardly on his tongue.

"Yeah." Harrow stepped closer, boots silent on the alloy. "You soak up the CEO's orders. Absorb his suspicions. Take in all the little secrets he doesn't want to dirty his hands with. He keeps you on hand like a cached file until it's time to decrypt. Then—" He twisted his hands, slow and deliberate. "— he wrings you out. You spill everything. And just like that, you're ready to soak up the next order. It's the same way they used recruits in the war—throw them into the substrate fields, let them soak up the fallout until they were spent, then replace them with fresh ones."

Keir stiffened. A pause. Then, tightly: "I don't understand you, sir."

Harrow laughed. No joy. No madness. Just exhaustion twisted into noise. "Good. A corrupt script runs unimpeded when the processor doesn't know it's been hacked."

Keir stepped forward, voice taut. "Enough. Tell us where the body is. The CEO is waiting."

Harrow's eyes glinted in the dark. "The body is with the CEO," he said. Each word deliberate. "But the CEO … is not with the body."

Keir frowned. "What does that mean?"

"The CEO is a thing," Harrow said, venom curling in his throat.

"A … thing?" Keir echoed.

"A placeholder," Harrow said, teeth flashing. "A ghost in a stolen shell."

He let the silence stretch. Outside, a drone whined past. Inside, only the hum of surveillance tech and the still air of unspoken dread.

The lights shimmered across Harrow's face. For a second, it seemed like he wasn't in sync with himself. Three versions of him flickered on the wall.

"Fine," he said. "Let's go see the king."

"You mean Viktor?" Keir asked.

"Yes, I mean Viktor," Harrow said, sharper. "Who else would I mean?"

Keir's frown deepened. He took Harrow by the arm and steered him down the hallway. The corridor stretched long and silent, light panels humming like a machine about to break.

They were almost to Viktor's executive suite when Cassandra appeared around the corner. She was pale, eyes wide, moving like someone who had been running but didn't remember when she'd stopped.

"Is it true?" Her voice cracked like glass.

Harrow flinched.

Tears formed before she could blink them back. "Viktor's signed the order. They're planning your execution in Neo-Paris."

Harrow's throat tightened. "Over Marr?"

She shook her head. "Even before Dad. This isn't new. You were always on the list."

Silence pressed in. The only sound was the filtered air hissing through the vents.

"Why are you telling me this?" he asked.

Her gaze faltered, fixed on the sterile floor. "I don't know. Maybe because no one ever warned *me*."

He turned to Keir. "Did you know?"

Keir's expression was unreadable, too smooth to trust. "No. I don't know what she's talking about."

Harrow studied him for a beat, then nodded slowly. He faced Cassandra again. "Thank you. I should get going. Wouldn't want to keep the High and Mighty waiting."

Their eyes locked. For a moment, the world narrowed to just the two of them, and he almost believed their old love could survive anything—even this machine, even death stamped in official ink.

The chamber was quiet.

Glass walls, empty chairs, mirrored floors. It wasn't that something had concluded. It was that something had begun.

Harrow stood alone at the center, his shadow long under the ceiling lights, cast like a judge waiting to deliver a verdict. The weight of Elsinore pressed inward—corporate, clinical, divine. This was no longer a company. It was the kingdom of a god. And it was watching him. Harrow muttered: "Yea, though I walk through the valley of corrupted servers, I shall fear no audit."

Across from him stood Viktor, with a composed expression, hands folded behind his back. To his left was Corra, her shoulders tense and her eyes fixed straight ahead.

To his right, Director Marr's absence engulfed the space like a black hole.

Viktor spoke first, his voice smooth and almost gentle, like velvet draped over steel.

"We regret it came to this. But your safety remains … our priority."

Harrow tilted his head, a half-smile twitching at his mouth.

"My safety?" he echoed, each syllable lacquered with disbelief.

"We believe time abroad will offer you clarity. Space. Perspective." Viktor's gaze was steady, practiced. He'd rehearsed this.

Harrow's smile widened—cold and sharp. "Perspective is for men unsure of what lies ahead."

Viktor didn't flinch. He straightened his back slightly, fingers circling the rim of his untouched glass.

"You leave tonight. Neo-Paris. A private escort. Arrangements are made."

Corra stirred—barely. The faint shift of fabric, the tremor of someone trying not to intervene.

"Neo-Paris still owes favors," Viktor went on. "Still remembers debts from before the firewalls went up. We'll see them honored."

The city was rebuilt on war debris—substrate silos gutted and repurposed into data vaults, black-market channels codified into law. Everyone there still carried the war in their bones, even if they sold it with polished smiles.

Harrow turned, slowly, to face her. "Mother," he said.

The word struck harder than any curse. The room seemed to lean in, listening.

"My mother," he repeated, the tone dropping colder, carved with ice. "Your title, not your right."

Corra swallowed against the silence—but the silence swallowed her back. She said nothing.

He looked back at Viktor, eyes lit with something colder than fire. "The ghost knows what you did."

Viktor didn't move. His reply came measured, balanced, the words carefully weighed. "Ghosts," he said evenly, "are only code. You of all people should know that."

"Yes," Harrow murmured. A blade of agreement turned sideways. "But sometimes decompiling corrupted code reveals the truth."

Above them, the lights flickered—briefly exposing the steel ribs of the ceiling like bones beneath skin. Harrow stepped forward. Close enough that Viktor could feel the weight of his breath, the heat of a body charged with defiance.

"We were supposed to be a family," he said, each word cut from glass.

Viktor's jaw shifted, just enough to betray the calculation behind his calm. "We are a legacy."

Harrow blinked slowly, as if giving him the chance to reconsider. Then his mouth curved into something thin and sharp. "Wrong noun."

He straightened, tugged once at the cuff of his sleeve, smoothing his coat.

"Well," he said, voice light but dangerous at the edges. "If I am to be banished, let it be with flair."

He turned toward the door. Paused. Pivoted back, eyes locked on Viktor like a hunter savoring the final moment before release.

"At dinner," Harrow said softly, almost kindly, "tell them you ate well. That the son you raised made a toast. That he left smiling." He let the silence hang. Then, a beat later, added: "Tell them I forgave you."

He bowed—deep, formal, exaggerated enough to mock the gesture. It was theater. It was war.

Then, without another word, he walked out, his shadow dragging long across the floor.

The doors closed behind him, sealing with a hush that felt louder than a gunshot.

Viktor remained still. He didn't shift, didn't breathe, as though motion itself might unspool the control he'd just maintained. Corra sat in a chair—one hand flexing against her gown's fabric—but no words came. Not yet.

There had been other ways. Quieter routes. Louder routes. Bloodier routes. But none so efficient. None so final.

At last, Viktor turned to the waiting security aide at the edge of the room. The man stood rigid, eyes locked forward, as if afraid to witness what he already knew.

"Neo-Paris," Viktor said, his voice stripped of ceremony. "Make sure he doesn't come back."

It was the same phrasing commanders used in the Substrate War when sending soldiers into no-return campaigns—clean orders for dirty deaths. Efficiency disguised as mercy.

The aide dipped his head once, sharp and wordless. Orders received. Sentence carried.

Only then did Corra find her voice. It cracked through the silence like a flaw in glass. "He'll know."

Viktor didn't look at her. He kept his eyes fixed on the empty space where Harrow had stood. "He already does."

Outside, thunder cracked over the city—rolling deep through the neon-lit canyons. The sound echoed like the slow collapse of something vast and unfixable.

Viktor stood motionless, waiting for the lightning that never came.

Thunder crackled as the hovercar glided over the upper grid, neon billboards spilling their colors onto the rain-slick glass, rippling in shallow waves along the windshield. Harrow leaned back against the seat, jaw slack, eyes tracking upward through the transparent roof as the spires of Elsinore rose and warped into glass spears, stabbing at a cloud-smeared sky. Their edges caught the light in sharp flashes, cold and exact.

The Neon breathed without lungs, a perpetual-motion organism of steel and signals, built on feedback loops, automation, and the inertia of deals struck in sealed rooms. It didn't pause to consider what it had become; it just kept running the program, iteration after iteration, refining only the perpetuation of its own existence.

Next to him, the security officer sat with his hands folded in his lap, giving off the vibe of someone on a routine assignment. His voice—when he spoke—lacked a distinguishable accent, tailored to sound like it came from nowhere and everywhere. His uniform lacked any insignia, erasing any indication of rank or allegiance.

Up front, Keir sat stiffly in the passenger seat, his profile illuminated in alternating pulses of pink and green as the Neon glared through gaps in the skyline. His gaze never wavered from the horizon, fixating on the maze of streetlights and shadows far below. The driver—another corporate ghost dressed in black—kept the throttle steady, the engine's hum rising into a relentless drone. The car didn't slow.

"You spoke well," the officer said. "To Viktor."

Harrow didn't respond. The light shifted. Billboards blinked out slogans he no longer read.

The officer continued. "Do you believe in loyalty?"

"Not in yours," Harrow said.

A pause. The car turned, silent as breath.

"There's nothing left in this city but mirrors and reflections," Harrow said. "None of them aligned. All of them blinking out of sync. Like ghosts performing routines they never chose."

The officer gave a small nod. "Is that why you provoked him?"

"I didn't provoke him. I revealed him."

Silence stretched. The hum of the hover system whispered under it.

Harrow leaned forward, resting his forehead against the cold glass. The skyline flickered past like a dying signal. He mouthed words without sound, an old prayer he no longer believed in. *Lord, remember my father.* The words hung dead in the glass, unanswered. All these towers. All these wires. All these people who had sold their souls for the comfort of compliance.

"My father died for nothing," he said. "And they recorded it. Labeled it a fault in the system. And I? I was expected to forget. To recalibrate."

He exhaled sharply. "They said the Substrate War was over, but all it did was migrate—from fields of substrate and ash to the marrow of our families. Every casualty redrafted as a statistic. Every betrayal archived as strategy. Even my father's end was logged like another wartime casualty."

The officer said nothing. His silence was perfectly measured.

"He had a war inside him," Harrow said. "And I wasn't there. I missed it. I missed him. I wanted him back so badly, I took the ghost. I listened to code dressed up like soul."

He closed his eyes.

"I asked myself why I didn't kill Viktor when I had the chance."

The officer tilted his head.

"What flaw in my design made the kill command stall in my

throat? What ghost-code error looped inside me, keeping me soft when the system demanded steel?"

He opened his eyes. Looked down at his own hands.

"My father had a war inside him," he repeated. "And me? Just silence."

The car slowed. The platform ahead blinked into focus.

He pushed off the window and sat straighter. Something behind his eyes had changed.

There was no more need to search. Only to strike. No more simulations. Just the act. His father had begged. He would not. His war would not be whispered.

"Where are we?" Harrow asked.

The officer turned to him. "The staging point. From here, you go to Neo-Paris."

"And from there?"

The officer smiled faintly. "Wherever they send people they'd rather forget."

Harrow nodded.

"I'll remember that."

The car docked. The door hissed open. He stepped out.

Behind them, the city carried on—efficient, eternal, blind to the war blooming in its core. The Substrate War had ended twenty-five years ago, but its logic had metastasized into Elsinore itself: everything optimized, everything expendable, even memory.

Even the protests—a restless knot of bodies at the tower's base—barely registered, just another line item on the city's operating ledger. The chants below rose and fell like a litany, sounding like prayer but beseeching no god.

CHAPTER 20

"When an architect of order is removed, stabilize by removing the anomaly."

—CRISIS CONTAINMENT MANUAL, LINE OF SUCCESSION SUBROUTINE 3.2

Rook didn't cry. He didn't scream. Didn't throw a punch. Didn't put a hole in the wall or demand footage or ask Reynaldo for a second version of the story—one with a cleaner ending. One that didn't leave him standing here with nothing in his hands but an echo of truth.

He just stood there.

The rain slid down the inside of his collar, cold as ice, but he didn't move. The alley smelled like oil and ash and piss, a chemical rot that clung to the back of his throat. The glow from the broken overhead sign kept flickering *MIND THE STATIC // MIND THE STATIC* in half-lit pulses, strobing the space in sick intervals, making everything feel like it was happening out of sync.

His jaw ached. He still tasted blood—from biting too hard, from choking back the anger that wanted to explode.

Reynaldo shifted near the mouth of the alley, soaked to the bone, his boots making soft sucking sounds in the film of runoff and gutter oil. He had flown to Neo-Paris himself to deliver the news. Had volunteered. Then he said the words.

"It was Harrow."

Three words. A sentence like a knife slipped between vertebrae, neat and surgical. That's how you kill someone like Rook—not with steel, but with the burden of betrayal.

"Christ…"

"He didn't fight back," Reynaldo added after a beat, voice barely carrying over the rain. "Not that they could tell."

The flicker from the sign washed over Rook's face again. Static. Static. Static. And still, he didn't move.

Rook breathed out—a slow, rattling exhale, like the air in his lungs had spoiled. "Was it clean?"

"No." Reynaldo's gaze slid away, finding something else to watch in the dark. "Stabbed him through a curtain. Close range. Front of the body."

That sat between them, heavy as ballast, long enough for the rain to change pitch against the alley's metal siding. Long enough for Rook's fingers to loosen from his clenched fists. His hands were shaking. He only noticed when the rain tapped off his palms like he was holding something alive.

"People keep asking me," Rook said finally, voice low and flat, "if I ever hated Dad."

Reynaldo turned his head, eyes narrowing in the flicker-light. "Did you?"

"I used to." Rook nodded once, sharp, as if the motion alone could cut the past clean. "For making me into him. For training me like a weapon instead of raising me like a son. For giving me steel where I should've had skin. For teaching me how to take a life before I knew what it was worth. He called it training. I called it sin."

The neon overhead caught in his eyes, hard and bright as polished steel.

"But now?" he said. "Now I just want him back."

He swallowed hard. "He came out of the Substrate War thinking he'd beaten it—thinking he'd carved a little order out of chaos. But the war never left him. It lived in his bones, and he passed it on like inheritance. That was his legacy. And mine."

Reynaldo didn't speak. He didn't have to. The broken sign buzzed overhead, pulsing *MIND THE STATIC // MIND THE STATIC*, until it was the only sound left between them.

Rook straightened slowly, vertebrae clicking. "You know what gets me?"

Reynaldo's voice was cautious. "What?"

"I trusted Harrow." The words had a jagged edge, his voice cracking from the sheer absurdity of it. "After everything—after the lies, the angles, the games—I still trusted him."

Silence engulfed the alley, stretching between the flickers of the busted sign.

Rook turned, pulling his hood up against the rain. The gesture was pointless; the rain had already found its way under his skin, cold and deep, soaking him from the inside out.

"Find me everything Dad was working on before he died," he said, low but clear. "Every file. Every dead drop. I don't care how encrypted, how buried, how many keys it takes to open. If even a shadow of Harrow touched it, I want to see it."

"And then?" Reynaldo asked.

Rook didn't look back. The rain plastered his hood to his skull, drumming a steady, hollow beat.

"Then," he said, "I'm going to bury him."

CHAPTER 21

"If there is a record of wrongdoing, bury it. The legacy must proceed."

—Brand Continuity Guide, Internal Ethics Hack 6.0

Beyond the walls, the Versailles Tower was a riot of boots, shouting, and alarms. Protesters had broken through. In the chaos, Harrow had slipped free of Keir and the ones sent to kill him. Out there, Harrow Eisler was already dead. In here, surrounded by the ghosts of a thousand purged files, he could choose to be a dead man—quiet and buried, or undead and clawing back up through the code and dragging the living down with him.

Harrow stood in an auxiliary data room—a steel box with no windows, no exits save the one that had just vanished behind him. Rows of servers lined the walls, emitting heat and the faint metallic tang of recycled air. Every breath felt borrowed.

Encrypted consoles washed his face in cold blue light, etching the stubble and the sleepless red in his eyes. Cipher streams crawled across the screens like restless insects, alive but oblivious to him.

He pulled up an interface, a relic from the Elsinore Analytics war archive—a system first built during the Substrate War, when kill-orders were logged like troop movements, neat entries in a database pretending to be history. Inherited, buried, then repurposed in this rusty embassy bunker. He typed the access code with a slight tremor: VKR-THV-999. The system hesitated, then blinked to life.

Access granted.

Security level: Director.

The execution order was already queued. Drafted weeks ago, signed by Viktor, and uploaded to the central judicial vault. It was a perfect death sentence: neat, self-contained, irreversible. Harrow's name was etched at the top. He almost laughed. A eulogy without a prayer. No priest, no psalm—just a line of code consigning him to oblivion. Exactly the same way soldiers and civilians had once been consigned to die for substrate, their names reduced to strings in the same ledger of expendables.

He stared at it for a long moment.

"Funny," he murmured. "They killed a version of me I hadn't become yet."

He brought up the override script. His fingers moved more slowly now, more deliberately. This wasn't a deletion. Deletions left traces. Rewriting it—*transforming* it—required surgical precision and careful elegance.

He changed the target from *Subject: Harrow Eisler* to *Subject: Keir Tavant*. A scapegoat. Blood for blood, code for code. Harrow left the rest of the metadata unchanged. The order would go through automatically. It would be executed by someone halfway around the world who wouldn't notice the difference. Just not on him.

The entire transaction had been routed through at least three former Elsinore blacksites and a now-defunct mining colony on Titan. Half of those nodes were built on the ruins of war infrastructure—bunkers where substrate once bled the world dry, now rebranded as secure server farms. He scrubbed his digital trail through this wilderness. By the time anyone found the fingerprints, he'd be dust.

The screen flickered. Then the order refreshed.

STATUS: Modified

EXECUTION TARGET: TAVANT, KEIR

ORDER AUTHORIZED BY: HECTOR MARR, DIRECTOR

Harrow leaned back in the chair, exhaling as if he'd been holding his breath since New Vienna. The silence closed in again, but this time it felt … thinner. Less permanent.

He switched the screen off.

And for the first time in months, he let himself whisper: "I want to live."

Not for justice. Not for revenge. Not even for redemption.

But because somewhere, in the burned-out wreckage of the world they'd built, someone still called him by name — not his code, not his title. Just *Harry*.

And that was enough to rewrite fate.

CHAPTER 22

"Your mind is a proprietary asset. If compromised, report to Human Resources."

—Elsinore Handbook, Section 8.2.1: Cognitive Integrity Clause

Cassandra walked down a corridor that buzzed like it had a fever. The overhead fluorescents flickered sporadically, casting pale, epileptic shadows across the exposed conduit and damp concrete. Somewhere far below, beyond the tower's barriers, the protest lines still held, their chants reduced to a dull throb through the steel bones of the building. Cassandra paused at the access panel, the pulse in her temple syncing up with the throbbing in the walls. She pressed her palm to the reader. Nothing.

She didn't try again right away. Were they watching?

Her free hand dug into her coat pocket, thumb running over the smooth, worn ridges of her Saint Expeditus coin. She rubbed the edge until it burned, a habit left over from childhood.

The panel mocked her; the access light stubbornly remained red. It might be betraying her, alerting them to her presence. Her heart raced, she looked around, then pulled herself together. She placed her hand on the panel. The light turned green.

The door emitted the tired hiss of hesitant submission. It swung open with a mechanical sigh, as if exhausted from admitting people.

Pax was already inside.

He stood near the back of the room, half-lit by the failed light grid above, his silhouette defined more by absence than presence. Leaning against a gutted server bank, he looked like someone born from shadow—shoulders relaxed, one foot crossed over the other, arms folded across his chest in the posture of a man who knew waiting was part of the job. No uniform. No comm relay. No pistol. Just him. Watchful. Composed. An old scar curled just beneath his left eye, barely visible unless you were looking for it. Cassandra was.

She stepped over the threshold.

"You're early," she said. Her voice came out louder than she intended.

Pax tilted his head. "You're late."

He didn't smile. He never smiled except to disarm someone. And this moment did not require disarmament.

Cassandra's hands hovered, then fumbled—tugging at the hem of her coat, smoothing the fabric along her ribs, again and again. Three passes. She counted them without meaning to, then made herself stop.

The overhead lights buzzed louder inside the chamber. Or maybe it was just her. Her pulse had been misfiring for days now, like her heart was trying to decide whether to fight or flee. Some nights it galloped until her vision stuttered. Other nights, it slowed to a crawl, as if even her blood had grown tired.

She didn't sleep anymore. She napped in fifteen-minute stretches, always dressed, sometimes with her boots still on.

"I brought it," she said, willing her voice to be steady, as she reached into the folds of her coat and withdrew a shard wrapped in silver mesh. The wrap crackled faintly in her gloved hand, sensitive to heat and static. "It's all in here. Procurement records. Trial protocols. The … the personnel changes they made when Viktor took control of—"

Her tongue caught. The words slid out of reach mid-sentence like she'd left them in another room.

She blinked once. Twice. Closed her eyes tight and drew a long, slow breath, as though trying to force her thoughts into a single file line. Reboot the moment.

"Sorry," she murmured. "I had it all in my head. The way I was going to say it."

Pax didn't move. Didn't speak right away. Just watched her with his quiet, calculating eyes. Not unkind. But cautious. Like he was assessing the situation.

"You okay?" he asked.

She barked a laugh—short, sharp, unconvincing. "Of course not. But don't worry—" Her eyes flashed, and for a heartbeat, they looked fever-bright. "I'm lucid."

She set the shard down on the crate between them—gently, as if it were fragile, even though it was built to withstand EMP bursts and take on firewalls so dense they almost had a mind of their own. Shards like this had first been issued in the Substrate War, carrying kill-lists and troop rotations with encryption that even governments couldn't crack. Now Elsinore used the same tech to shuffle budgets and silence dissent. Her hands stayed on the cold metal, fingers twitching, reluctant to pull away.

"Quantum encryption," she said. Her voice had gone clinical now, rehearsed. "You'll need to isolate it before opening. Don't let it touch anything neural. There's … there might be signatures."

Pax narrowed his eyes. "Might be?"

Cassandra's gaze flicked past him to the wall, unfocused. She didn't answer immediately.

"I've been seeing things," she said at last, the words almost apologetic. "In the code. In the lights. Shapes that aren't supposed to move." Her brow knitted. "But they do. They crawl across the margins like … like notes in a song no one taught me. I think it's a glitch. Or maybe—"

She pulled back and shook her head. Her hair, slightly damp from the humidity, stuck to the side of her face.

"Doesn't matter," she said softly, but she didn't believe it.

Pax remained silent. The space between them grew tense, heavy with all she wasn't saying. When he finally spoke, his voice was soft and cautious.

"Why me?"

Cassandra blinked slowly, as if the question needed translation. Then she pressed her teeth firmly against the inside of her cheek, her jaw tightening noticeably. A faint trace of red appeared at the corner of her mouth.

"Because you still believe in something," she said. "And I've forgotten how."

Pax reached for the shard. His fingers brushed the mesh. It felt warm—residual body heat from her holding it too long, too tightly. He turned it over slowly, watching the embedded light threads flicker like a beating heart.

"You were going to go public."

"I *was*. I wrote the post six times. Different voices. Different angles. Full disclosure, just-the-facts, even tried poetic once. But it felt like shouting into a vacuum. Like the Feed had walls trying to lock me away."

Her eyes darted toward the ceiling, then to the corners of the room, as if someone was watching. She flinched as shadows danced in the flickering light.

"I can't tell what's real anymore, Pax. I hear things at night. Music sometimes. My mother's voice, calling from the hallway. She sings the same song over and over." Her lips curved in a broken smile, caught somewhere between nostalgia and reality. "She's been dead twelve years."

Pax stepped toward her, slowly. Measured. He didn't reach for her, but his presence felt like a wall standing between her and the jagged edge.

"Cass," he said gently, "maybe we should get someone—"

"No." She cut him off with a suddenness that startled him. "No, this is the moment. Right here. This is me doing the right thing. Finally."

She pressed her palm against the surface of the crate where the shard had been, as if to ground herself.

"Even if I'm … broken. Even if I'm not enough."

Her voice cracked on that last part—revealing the depth of her pain.

She turned to leave, her coat swishing softly behind her. Pax raised his hand instinctively, letting it hang in the space between them—but he didn't touch her, just hovered there, uncertain.

"If something happens—" he began.

Cassandra paused at the door, her silhouette limned in flickering light. She didn't look back.

"It already did," she whispered.

Then she was gone. The door slid shut behind her with an echo of finality. Pax stood alone with the silence.

CHAPTER 23

"Erasure is the cruelest weapon. To kill a man is to stop him; to
erase him is to expunge all memory of his existence."

— ARCHIVIST'S COMMENTARY, SUBSTRATE WAR REMNANTS

The return from Neo-Paris was always jarring. Rook stepped out
of the Auto-Cab and into the hollow arteries of Elsinore Tower.
The sound shifted immediately—the metallic roar of a foreign city
fading into the soft, steady hum of home. The air was cooler here,
thinner, tinged faintly with sterilizers and recycled oxygen. His coat
still carried the weight of foreign rain and the scent of street smoke
in its seams, but already the tower's air was beginning to strip it away.

Pax was waiting. He didn't pace, didn't fidget. He stood at the
far end of the corridor, like a man built into the wall; his stillness a
quiet rebuke to the world's restlessness. Only his eyes shifted when
Rook approached.

"You're back."

Rook stopped a few feet away. The words should have been nothing, a simple acknowledgment, but they pressed down heavier than his pack. He hadn't realized until that moment how tired he was, how much Neo-Paris had worn him down and left him behind. His voice came out flat. "The city hasn't changed," he said. "Just me."

"Neo-Paris does that." Pax tilted his head, eyes measuring, as if confirming what he already suspected. He had the patience of a priest waiting for a confession. "We need to talk about Cassandra."

Her name hit harder than he expected. Rook felt the words drop inside him like a stone sinking into still water, sending ripples that stiffened his spine and tightened every muscle. "What about her?"

"She's unsettled. Edgy." Pax's tone remained steady, but it carried a cautious weight, as if each syllable was placed with deliberate precision. "When I saw her last, she pressed a shard into my hand. Encrypted."

Rook's mouth went dry, with a metallic taste rising at the back of his throat. "She gave it to you?"

"She trusted me to pass it on."

His jaw moved once, then again. "That isn't like her," he said finally. "Cassandra doesn't hand off her secrets unless she's running. And if she's running, it's not from the dark. It's from someone."

"Which is why I thought you should know." Pax's voice remained calm, but the air around him seemed thicker for it. "She's trying to put out too many fires. One of them will burn her."

Rook ran a hand over the ridges of his arm, alloy cool and unforgiving beneath his touch. The gesture wasn't comforting; it was grounding. He said nothing. The silence stretched, tight as a wire, humming with everything he couldn't put into words.

It was Pax who broke the silence. "And what about Harrow?"

The name hit harder than the shard, even more than Cassandra's uncomfortable silence. It bore weight like iron.

"What about him?" Rook asked, though he already knew.

"You know what. He killed Marr."

The words hit like shrapnel, and Rook flinched before he could stop himself. Marr's absence was everywhere—not just in memory, but in the fabric of the Tower itself. The corners that should have been guarded by his father's shadow stood bare. The dossiers that should have borne his handwriting arrived in cold, unfamiliar fonts. Even silence had changed timbre without his presence to fill it.

"I know," Rook finally said. His throat clenched around the words, tearing them raw. "And I'm furious enough to kill him for it."

"That won't heal you." Pax's tone was steady, but underneath it ran a wave of grief, held back like a blade kept in its sheath.

"It doesn't need to heal *me*." Rook's cybernetic hand clenched into a fist against his thigh, the sound of metal tendons straining. "It needs to end *him*."

Pax stepped forward, allowing the light to cast his shadow across the corridor floor. "You kill him, and Viktor wins. You know that."

Rook's gaze locked onto his, steady and intense, like the chamber of a loaded gun. "Maybe. Maybe not. But I can't breathe while he still walks free."

For a long time, Pax held him in that stare, searching for any fault line—a tremor in his jaw, a slip in his voice, anything to force reason in. But Rook offered nothing. He stood like stone, anger keeping him upright.

"Don't try to stop me," Rook said.

"I won't," Pax murmured. There was no surrender in it, only inevitability. "But you'll regret it."

The corridor stretched ahead, sterile and long, lined with glass that reflected nothing. Rook turned away from him and walked into it, his shadow growing sharper with each step, carrying his anger like a blade already drawn.

The words didn't just wound; they hollowed.

There would be no funeral. There couldn't be. Harrow made sure of that. Whatever was left of Marr—body, records, even the comfort of remains—had been destroyed. Erased. Rook wasn't even allowed the ritual of standing over his father's grave, nor a handful of dirt to mark the end. There was nothing to bury. Nothing to keep. Nothing to say goodbye to.

Rook had tried to shoulder it, just as Marr would have wanted. Straight back, steady step, no weakness for anyone to see. But grief bent him from the inside. Grief made him raw. And Harrow— Harrow had done this.

That was what shattered him. Not just the death, but the erasure. Harrow hadn't only killed his father. He'd taken him from memory, erased him as if he had never existed.

And Harrow had been his friend. Closer than blood, once—the boy who'd stood beside him when the rest of the Tower turned its back, the voice he trusted when he trusted no one else. Rook had believed in him. Believed *with him*.

But friends don't erase fathers. Friends don't burn the body and leave you with nothing but shadows.

"I want to kill him," Rook said. The words came out heavy, stripped of heat, stripped of threat. Just truth.

But the Tower gave him nothing in return. No answer. No echo. Marr was gone, and nothing Rook did—no fury, no vengeance—would bring him back. The thought landed heavier than anger, heavier than blame. It was all that was left to him.

He bowed his head. For a moment, alloy and flesh both felt useless, powerless against the emptiness that spread and held.

CHAPTER 24

"Contracts can be broken, and bonds can be severed. Protocol must be preserved."

—SECURITY INTEGRITY MEMO, RELATIONSHIP COMPLIANCE CLAUSE 11-C

That morning, Corra and Pax waited outside the med chamber like mourners at the door of a tomb.

Corra stood rigid, back straight, shoulders tight, attempting to keep grief from leaking out. She had the trained stillness of her class. No trembling. Not in public. Not where it could be weaponized. Her hands hung at her sides—numb.

Pax leaned against the far wall, arms crossed casually, ankle resting over the opposite foot. But his stance was a lie. The line of his shoulders betrayed him. His eyes flicked down the corridor every few seconds, cataloging exits, mapping threats. As if the walls themselves might turn hostile. As if the system might take back what little mercy it had offered.

The door hissed.

The medic stepped out. Middle-aged, pallid, hands twitching faintly as if he didn't know where to put them. He opened his mouth. Closed it again. Then:

"She's awake," he said. "But not … well."

The pause spoke volumes.

He stepped aside.

Corra went in first, her heels muted against the sterile floor. She hadn't changed out of the executive black, but it hung differently now—creased, tired, as though the power weave of the fabric had gone dormant.

Cassandra sat on the edge of the medbed, upright but swaying slightly, like a marionette with a broken string. Her legs dangled, bare feet just above the floor. Her hair was loose, a dark spill down her back. Lips cracked. Eyes wild. Her pupils twitched like corrupted optics. Electrodes clung to her temples, blinking faint green and red.

She was humming. A phrase. Off-key. Off-tempo. But insistent.

Corra moved slowly, each step measured, unsure whether Cassandra was about to collapse or explode.

Cassandra turned toward her.

"I know you," she said, tilting her head. Her voice was high, musical. "You played queen. Very well, too. Even your lies were elegant."

Corra stopped mid-step. Something flickered in her face—grief, regret, recognition. Maybe all three. She said nothing.

Cassandra smiled. A strange, delicate curve of the lips with no warmth in it. Like someone remembering human emotion but not feeling it.

"They asked me where Harrow went," she said, sing-song. "I said I didn't know. I lied. I lie now. I lied then. I was full of lies, but he loved me anyway."

She plucked at a sensor cord like a child toying with string.

"They say I betrayed him," she murmured. "But it was my father. My father. They whispered into my ears—algorithms of betrayal. Error correction, they said. Clean code. Optimization."

The rhythm shifted. She began to sing softly, barely above a whisper.

"They logged me in with sugar words,
A promise in the shell—
But every vow is just a script
That terminates in hell."

Corra drew closer, a single chair separating her from the bed. She sat, hands folded carefully in her lap, then reached out, slow and tentative, toward Cassandra's shoulder.

She hesitated.

And withdrew.

Cassandra watched the hand retreat with cool amusement.

"Mother," she said. "Is that what I should call you? Lady of the mirrors? Queen of the frame?"

Her tone wasn't mocking. It was detached. Cataloging.

"We didn't mean for this," Corra said. Her voice cracked on the last word, too quiet for anyone but Cassandra to hear.

Cassandra laughed. Just once. Sharp and sudden.

"No one ever does. The system just ... wants. It consumes. It eats the best and praises the worst. And you—you fed it. You helped it eat him."

Pax stepped inside, silent as a shadow. His eyes flicked from Cassandra to Corra, then down to the floor. He stayed near the wall, as if his presence might tip the balance.

Cassandra tilted her head again. "Harrow said the system was built to lie. That Elsinore has no soul."

She paused.

"He was wrong."

Her voice dropped to a whisper.

"It has one. It just isn't human."

And then the song returned.

"*He touched my face with firelight code,*
And called my glitch divine—
But love was just a backdoor key
In someone else's spine."

Pax flinched.

Barely.

But enough for Cassandra to see.

Corra swallowed hard. "Cassandra, please. What do you want?"

Cassandra's eyes snapped back to her. For the first time, there was focus in them. Cold and absolute.

"I want the world to burn clean," she said. "I want the ghosts to speak. I want the dead to log back in."

Her hand moved—no warning, no hesitation—and found Corra's wrist.

Her grip was gentle. But electric.

"I want you," she said, "to stop pretending we can go back."

Corra opened her mouth. Closed it. No words to betray her.

She stood. Nodded once to the medic, who stood ready, bracing for violence. He moved toward the sedative.

Cassandra leaned back against the bedframe as the hum of the machinery rose around her. She whispered as the drug took hold:

"So bury me in zeroes now,

Encrypt me in the stream.

The system keeps the waking world—

I'll haunt them in the dream."

Her eyelids drifted down.

The monitors steadied.

She didn't look peaceful.

She looked exiled.

More than broken.

Not mad—in need of debugging.

Not malfunctioning—just incompatible with the lie.

The corridor outside the hospital room was sterile and quiet, humming faintly with the energy suspended in time. Monitors beeped behind the door, muffled. Somewhere down the hall, a nurse called for an assist, her voice distant, irrelevant.

Corra stepped out first, her movements unsteady but poised. The sharp lines of her suit were creased now, her lipstick faintly smudged at the corner. She held her hands tightly, as if afraid they'd start shaking.

Viktor waited just outside the door, leaning against the wall with calculated calm. His arms were folded, his face like carved stone—cold, impenetrable, unbothered. But his eyes flicked to her, sharp and fast, reading her.

"She said Harrow left a message," Corra said. Her voice was raw. She didn't look at him.

Viktor straightened. "She is not well," he said. "We have to assume her account is compromised."

From the far end of the corridor, a shape moved—a shadow dislodging itself from the wall.

Rook.

He stepped forward, slow and deliberate. His coat hung open, one hand in the pocket, the other curled into a fist. He had been listening.

Viktor turned to him, ready for confrontation and welcoming it.

"She needs protection," he said. "I believe you can offer it."

Rook didn't speak right away. His jaw tensed. When he did speak, his voice was low, sharp as wire.

"What did you do to her?"

Viktor didn't flinch. "What was necessary."

Corra let out a breath—barely a sound, but it carried weight. She didn't step between them. Didn't defend him. She just stood there.

Rook took another step forward. His eyes hadn't left Viktor's. "You drugged her. You buried her. And now you want me to trust you to keep her safe?"

"She's not buried," Viktor said. "She's being preserved. Until the moment she can be of use to herself again."

"That's not your call."

"It's the call that is keeping her alive."

Rook didn't blink. The air between them was tense, electric. It stank of antiseptic, recycled air, and the bitter guilt posing as an act of kindness.

Viktor took a step closer. So close that Rook could have drawn a blade and ended it in one clean motion.

"You think me a villain," Viktor said. "Perhaps I am. But the system survives because I do what must be done. Not what I want. Not what is fair. What the system needs."

He raised a hand as if offering to surrender.

"If I'm guilty," he said, "take my life. Here. Now. No resistance."

A bold opening gambit. Clean, polished, strategic.

Rook stared at him. He didn't draw. He didn't move. But his posture shifted—slightly, almost imperceptibly. Analyzing the game, looking for the best counter-move.

"If I'm innocent," Viktor went on, "then help me find the one who isn't."

Corra watched them both. Her face was unreadable now. She had folded herself back into armor, the CEO's widow, the executive queen. But her eyes seemed fragile.

Rook said nothing.

Viktor nodded once, satisfied with silence, and walked away, smooth and unrushed. In his mind, the game was already won.

CHAPTER 25

"Knowledge is power. Privacy is treason."

—Elsinore Surveillance Protocol, Justification Clause 7.2

The office still smelled like Marr. Not the man but the scent his filters left behind. Synthetic sandalwood, low-resin antiseptic, ozone.

Marr always kept the office meticulously clean. Everything was functional. No mementos, nothing personal that might lead to compromise. Always wiped down as if to remove any evidence.

Rook closed the door and engaged the manual lockout.

The security system recognized his iris. It knew the tilt of his jaw, the length of his stride. Recognized him as the rightful successor. The desk lights rose automatically. The screens hummed to life in perfect order.

He hated how seamless it was.

The terminal blinked once, then opened under his authorization. He scanned for an internal directory where Marr kept records he deemed too confidential or damning to write to the system memory banks.

A directory of personal logs appeared:

DIR.MARR.PARENTAL_OVERRIDE

DIR.MARR.SURV.COMP

DIR.MARR.HARROW.EXE

Rook stared at the last one.

He should have gone for it. Should have opened the files on Harrow. Found the evidence. Justified the anger.

Instead, he opened the first.

Playing entry 001 …

The screen filled with grainy footage: a boy, eight years old, sitting straight-backed at a reinforced desk. Wearing a stiff suit two sizes too big for him.

Marr's voice—flat, instructive—filled the speakers.

"*Lesson one: Emotion is not a core process. Filter it. Route it. Make it useful.*"

The boy nodded. He didn't speak.

"*You don't need to speak to be understood. You only need to be intelligible.*"

Rook shut off the file.

He poured himself a drink from the cabinet beneath the desk. Marr's drink. 80-proof ceramic-filtered gin with a citrus trace and no lingering finish.

The silence in the room changed after that.

It deepened and punctuated his actions.

Rook tapped into the second directory. Surveillance overlays.

Memos. Shadow copies of private conversations. Cassandra. Harrow. Corra. His own reports, annotated in Marr's voice.

He hadn't known about half of it.

There was a clip of Harrow and Cassandra kissing in a hospital stairwell.

There was another of Cassandra crying in the elevator, alone, mouthing his name.

There was a record of Marr's approval:

"*Cassandra's attachment is strong. Harrow's guilt will weaponize it. Allow the connection to deepen—temporarily.*"

Rook didn't flinch.

Didn't breathe.

He stared at the timestamp. Ten days before the gala.

His father had been engineering her grief in advance.

Another file. Audio only.

"*If he turns on us, we'll bury him in sentiment. Let him drown in her absence. It's more elegant than force and leaves no record.*"

Rook turned the volume down. Not off. Just … distant.

A surveillance file labeled "odd behavior." The timestamp read June twenty-first, one in the morning. Security guards reacted to something in front of them, but there was nothing there. Then static. Now the timestamp said June twenty-second at three in the morning, and Pax was with them. Once again, they responded to something unseen. Again, static. The timestamp was just after midnight on the twenty-third. Pax, a security guard, and now Harrow, were clearly reacting to something the cameras could not capture. "Odd behavior" was an understatement.

Rook remembered the last thing Marr had said to him in this office.

"You're not ready."

He hadn't said goodbye.

Hadn't said *son*.

Just *not ready*.

Rook leaned back, staring up at the ceiling where the light was clean and sharp and left no room for ghosts.

He should have deleted the files. Purged them. Let his father vanish with dignity.

Instead, he flagged three folders for retention.

KEEP: MARR.LOG.REGRETS.ENC

KEEP: HARROW.INTERCEPT

KEEP: CASSANDRA/EXIT/FAILSAFE

He stared at that last one.

The failsafe was still active. A whisper protocol. A prewritten obituary. A lie for the feeds.

She hadn't triggered it. That told him more than anything else could.

Whatever was coming, she wasn't going to run.

Rook finished the drink.

Set the glass down.

Opened the file on Harrow.

CHAPTER 26

"The system does not mourn for obsolete hardware."

—End-of-Connection Protocol, Heartware Subdivision

Pax remained at Elsinore Analytics, a ghost in the system—haunting the corporate tower's labyrinthine data veins, sifting through encrypted feeds, ghost logs, and hidden subroutines.

He did not speak much. Did not act much. But he watched. And when he moved, the system paid attention.

In the days after Harrow's departure, there was silence. No directives. No damage reports. Just the hum of continued operations, like the machine had consumed him and filed the absence.

But Pax knew systems never forget. They process, store, and archive.

On the fourth day, a ghost ping appeared.

It came coded in an obsolete format, one used in the outer archipelagos before the orbital wars. A signature was buried in the noise, one Harrow had used only once. Before the academy. Before Pax ever conceived that his friend could be so dangerous.

He cracked the seal.

No sound. No animation. Just text.

Harry. Not Harrow. The voice before the edges were sharpened.

The message read like a burn log. Syntax corrupted. Punctuation fragmentary. But the tone came through clear enough:

I see now All of it It was never memory it was architecture A script we were made to speak And I got tired of delivering someone else's lines

But it's not enough to vanish Not anymore

There are ghosts in this code My father was one I became another And you—

You could be the firewall or the fuse

He signed it: *—Harry*

Then one word below it: *help*

Pax sat motionless for a long time.

He had seen the news feeds. Harrow's supposed reassignment. The silence from Neo-Paris. The falsified updates.

And now this.

Something about the phrasing cut sideways across his training. Harrow had always been sharp—but this was something else. Fragmented. Burning.

He keyed in a route to the executive wing. The screen glowed, steady and expectant, as though waiting for his reply. He sat with it a moment longer, the weight of Harrow's words pressing in like static that wouldn't clear.

On another floor in the Tower, the meditation alcove sealed behind Corra with a hiss too quiet to trust.

Blue light pulsed along the rim of the floor—Elsinore's branded shade of sterile calm, the same color they had first deployed in bunkers during the Substrate War, when soldiers were breaking and civilians begged for sedation. What had once been triage was now sold as therapy. The walls were seamless composites, matte and non-reflective until a sensor registered eye contact. There was no cross, no icon, no flame. Only an ergonomic bench patched with synthetic leather and a projection node that could simulate whatever higher power the user's neurology was most responsive to.

Corra lowered herself onto the bench. Its haptic stabilizers thrummed faintly against her spine, syncing posture to corporate ergonomics. For the first time in twelve hours, her shoulders sagged.

She had not cried. She had not spoken. She had not been asked.

But the alcove—this tiny, data-harvested cathedral of quiet—welcomed her with biometric calm. Her cortisol levels scrolled in ghost text across the projection node before fading into blue haze.

"*Welcome, Director Eisler,*" the AI intoned, voice as smooth as polished marble.

"*Your emotional load registers are elevated. Would you like to initiate the grief protocol? Premium empathy mode is available.*"

She closed her eyes. The system didn't seem to know she had remarried.

"No."

A pause, perfectly calculated to sound respectful. Then: "*Would you prefer mindfulness prompts or legacy-data journaling?*"

"I want to talk to my husband."

"*Silas Eisler is marked deceased. Would you like to access his memorial sequence? We offer three tiers: shared audio logs, private correspondence, digitized holographic simulation.*"

"No."

The walls adjusted their hue. Still. Waiting. Patient.

The AI generated a tone: three pulses per measure, mimicking a resting heartbeat. She hated that her nervous system obeyed it, cortisol tapering in real time.

"I just…" She pressed her hands against her knees. "I don't want a simulation. I want something real."

"*Define real,*" the AI prompted. Its tone never shifted.

She opened her eyes.

Her reflection looked back from the curved wall, already edited by photonic filters. The system softened her jawline, brightened her eyes, smoothed the shadows beneath them. Loss, rendered in corporate HDR. Somewhere in Elsinore's servers, her grief metrics were already archived.

"I think I made a mistake," she whispered.

The AI didn't respond. That phrase had no actionable outcome.

"I think I traded something that mattered for something I understood. And now I don't know how to reverse it."

The room logged her silence as distress. The blue dimmed further.

Outside the alcove, the Tower pulsed with system activity. Someone in PR was already drafting condolence statements. Somewhere, Viktor was sleeping—or pretending to. Somewhere, Harrow was burning out of orbit, and she had no idea how to reel him back.

"I thought … if I held it together long enough, the system would align. That the algorithms would balance the grief. That order would be enough."

She looked down at her hands. The alcove overlaid faint biometric tracers across her knuckles, ghost-blue lines marking pulse and skin conductivity.

"They're breaking," she said. "Both of them. Cassandra. Harrow. And I let it happen because I believed in the system more than I believed in them."

The AI recorded the statement, time-stamped it, flagged it for sentiment analysis.

She leaned forward, pressing her fingers to her temples, and whispered into the dark: "What if I chose the wrong ghost to follow?"

"*There is no recommended outcome for that input,*" the AI replied.

"Of course there isn't."

Her knees ached as she stood. The bench logged the weight change, flashing a polite *session ending detected.*

"I don't need a resolution," she said. "I just needed someone to hear me say it."

The panel lit under her hand.

"*Would you like to log this session to your internal record? Your data may be used to optimize future grief protocols.*"

She stared at the option.

[Y] [N]

She pressed N.

The door unsealed with another whisper.

She stepped into the corridor, wiped the corner of her eye with the back of her thumb, and walked away like nothing was cracked.

***

Across the city, the floating gardens orbited in perfect corporate symmetry over the black reservoir—once a war-scarred crater from the Substrate conflict, now paved over with bioluminescent code. Maintenance drones buzzed between them, their housings scarred with patchwork repairs, leaking coolant into the water below. Above, the dome glitched—constellations dissolving into pop-up ads before the system rebooted the illusion.

Cassandra stood barefoot on the edge of a floating platform, her boots neatly placed behind her in a broken ritual. The water beneath her reflected nothing. Just blackness. Still. Waiting.

She wrapped her arms around herself and exhaled. The air smelled of mineral water, synthetic pollen, ozone.

She soaked in the silence. This was the one place left in the city where the noise couldn't follow you—no feeds, no surveillance hum, no Harrow.

Even so, she thought she could still hear the faint chant of protestors outside the dome, filtered into static, like ghosts pressing against the glass.

She sat down. The platform's gridwork was cold against her thighs, laced with faint electric hum. The flowers around her were only nano-thread constructs, genetically sculpted into fragile approximations of life. They emitted scripted perfume in regular intervals, like programs looping in a broken prayer. Beautiful, but hollow.

Just like him.

Just like *her*, maybe.

He had looked her in the eye and lied. To him, it was a strategy, not a sin. And she—God, she had *defended* him. She had burned bridges for him, cracked passwords, betrayed ghosts. All for a man who traded trust and honor for utility. Used *love* as *leverage*.

"I would've followed you," she said. "Even then. Even after."

But he wouldn't let her follow. He just walked away.

It had taken a month to crack the divine firewall. Subtly injecting bits of code. Looking for vulnerabilities. Mapping unsecure ports. Unearthing forgotten root accounts. Waiting for the right time to exploit them all. She found that moment yesterday afternoon.

It wasn't built for mortals. The thing spoke in root-prayers and machine glossolalia; it dwelled above them. She had to trick it into believing she was part of the liturgy. That meant skin-bridging through her own spinal root, matching her pulse to the system, and slipping in the override during the half-breath between divine ping and human echo.

Two seconds. That was the window. Long enough to overwrite the failsafes. Clean. Untraceable. The neurobus didn't know it had been touched. Now it was too late to shut the door.

The hard part had been getting the tox-injector—no bigger than a stylus, all chrome and silence. An assassin's weapon. She'd spent a week tracking it down through darknet dead drops and air-gapped brokers, unsure if she'd ever use it. Maybe she just wanted to know she could. That the door wasn't locked. That it could be opened. That she could choose to step through.

She thought about including the hack in her files. Drop the logs, the access keys, the bypass sequence—gift-wrap it for the protesters so they could burn the whole architecture down from the spine up.

But hacking the divine firewall wasn't what they wanted. They wanted a villain they could name, a chain of signatures they could follow from crime to consequence. They wanted a narrative with an unambiguous resolution. They would see the hack as sacrilege. As punishment, they would be forced to face the horrors of free will.

She had hoped that cracking the firewall would ignite a blaze that would consume the chaff and drive out the plague-ridden rats getting fat at the top of the heap. But they wouldn't understand, wouldn't see the flame as an agent to forge a new future. In their panic, they would destroy themselves trying to stomp out the fire.

There would be no message. No data trail. No evidence buried in audio files. No trail to follow. He would search for meaning because that's what he did. He would claw through surveillance logs and sensor files. He would look for answers and only find questions. Maybe then he'd understand that what he broke could not be fixed. That some things don't come with second chances.

Cassandra held the injector to the base of her neck.

She didn't cry.

Instead, she smiled—small and real, like she used to before all this.

"It *was* love," she said softly. "But not enough."

Click.

The light in her eyes dimmed before the injector hit the metal floor.

Around her, the flowers kept blooming in synthetic cycles, their coded petals opening and closing to the rhythm of a machine that thought it was alive.

CHAPTER 27

The sky over the Neon was a bruised purple. Harrow stood motionless at the edge of Dock Three, shoulders hunched against the acrid wind that knifed between half-dead solar arrays and the rusted bones of scaffolding. The steel grating beneath his boots was slick with oil and rain, creaking and straining with each shifting breath of the wind, as if the city itself were restless.

Behind him, the Neon bled color: static-riddled signage, smeared red and sickly green. Half the shanties still wore scars from the Substrate War—walls patched with old ration tins, roofs soldered from surplus plating meant for soldiers who never came home. The war had ended a generation ago, but here its wreckage was still currency. The scent of ozone and rot—old batteries, burnt plastic, sweat, and worse.

Every few minutes, a cargo hauler roared up into the sky, its thrusters screaming against gravity. Thick-bellied things with no windows and no questions, disappearing into the roiling clouds like beasts returning to a nest. There were no passenger manifests. Just data. Sealed and sanctioned. Denial-proof.

Harrow clutched the data shard in his gloved hand, thumb grazing the beveled edge like he was testing its sharpness. He keyed it one last time. The execution order pulsed onto the retinal display—his name, erased. Keir's, inserted. Timestamped. Signed.

It had taken twelve seconds.

The consequences would last forever.

He slipped the shard back into the inside pocket of his coat and turned. The transit officer stood waiting under a flickering floodlamp, arms folded behind her back with the mechanical stillness of someone who'd long ago stopped caring. Her eyes were wet mirrors—optic implants that reflected his face back at him, distorted and stripped of warmth. The green of her uniform was faded. Her skin was the color of cold clay. She didn't smile. Elsinore employees never smiled this far down the chain.

"You're cleared," she said flatly. "One-way. Tower level. You'll dock at Platform Four."

Her voice had the rasp of low-grade vocal modification—cheap, industrial, lacking emotion or empathy.

"Cargo designation?" he asked.

Without ceremony, she handed him a small, matte-white hexagonal token. No barcode. No chip. Just enough authority to prevent the hauler from ejecting him mid-ascent.

"Medical waste," she said.

Harrow held it between his fingers, studying it.

He let out a breath that tasted like rust. "Fitting."

The officer didn't blink. Didn't nod. She merely stepped aside and gestured toward the hauler behind her—its belly open, the cargo ramp tilted down like a tongue leading to the inside of a mouth. Inside: darkness, silence, and the reek of formaldehyde.

The ship didn't care who he was.

He walked slowly, deliberately, like a man counting the steps to the gallows. Each footfall landed heavy on the steel, echoing in the hollow dark beneath the platform—slow, purposeful, steady, without cowardice. The cold bit through his coat now. He took no notice.

His mind replayed the moment he'd keyed the change. Fingers hovering over the command line. That blank screen waiting, cursor blinking like a question it already knew the answer to. He'd stalled—not long, just long enough to prove he'd thought about it. Long enough for the choice to stick.

It hadn't been strategy. Not a trade.

A confession.

He would live.

Keir wouldn't.

And he would return to Elsinore—to Viktor, to the Tower, to everything and everyone that knew exactly who he had become. The kind of man who writes a name in code over his own. Who starts a deadly countdown and lets it run.

He stopped at the threshold of the hauler.

The ramp beneath his feet was slick, its grip tread worn to dull nubs by years of freight transfers. The city pulsed behind him, the Neon snarling in reds and greens and a sick gold, like a fever dream trying to emerge. Somewhere far off, a siren wailed. Closer, a child laughed. And above it all, the towers blinked like indifferent gods.

The Neon had stripped him bare. Taken his father, his peace, his name. Turned him into something sharp and tired. And still, for all its hunger, it had left him this one, terrible thing:

A choice.

The trouble with choices is that they carry consequences. Long after you made them. Even after you stopped being the person who made them.

He stepped through the threshold into the ship's gut. He didn't look back.

The ramp retracted with a mechanical groan, sealing him in. The light died behind him.

And darkness swallowed him whole.

CHAPTER 28

"Executive death creates structural opportunity."

—Crisis Response Manual, CEO Succession Protocol v2.1

Viktor stood in his private suite, the city stretching out before him—neon grids and shadowed towers pulsed like the neural map of a living machine. Elsinore glowed below, a hive of power and obedience wrapped in the skin of progress. At its base, protesters knotted the avenues, their chants rising faintly even this high, static against the hum of the skyline. They carried slogans born from the Substrate War—the old demand that no system should decide whether a person lived or died. Viktor remembered when those chants first rose from the trenches; back then, they were drowned out by fire. Now, they echoed in the streets of his empire. He swirled amber liquor in a faceted crystal glass, watching the reflections fracture against the smart-glass windows. His own face stared back at him in fragmented overlay: controled, refined, unreadable.

Across from him, Rook sat rigid in a chrome-frame chair built for style rather than comfort. His eyes, still red-rimmed from grief, held a cold clarity. He was honing his rage into a weapon. His knee bounced slightly. His hands were ready, as if he were preparing to strike.

Viktor turned from the window, letting his voice roll smooth and tempered. "I want you to understand something. I had no hand in your father's death."

A pause. Measured. Strategic.

"You've heard the facts—Harrow, in a moment of madness, struck him down. Mistook him for me, Corra says."

Rook's jaw tightened. "Then why let him live?" he asked. "Why let a madman roam free after cold-blooded murder?"

Viktor exhaled, carefully performing the weariness of power— an emperor painted in shades of reluctant restraint. "Two reasons," he said. "Both critical."

He stepped closer to Rook.

"One: his mother. She is … indispensable to me."

The words lingered, quiet and raw, somewhere between confession and calculation.

"And two: the public."

He gestured toward the expanse beyond the glass, where light and shadow sprawled in artificial constellations. "They watch Harrow the way people watch collapsing stars—fearful, but unwilling to look away. They see tragedy and brilliance, not blood and instability. His pain absolves him. His lineage sanctifies him. If I moved against him openly, I would lose the people's trust." His voice hardened. "And perception is power, Rook. It builds kingdoms. It ends them."

Rook inhaled slowly. Something in him snapped into place. The rage was still there, but now it had structure. Shape. "And now?" he asked. "My father lies in a drone-sealed morgue. My sister..." He took a deep breath. "I went through all my father's files. Before his death, he was investigating Harrow. I didn't realize how dangerous he was until I read that file."

Viktor crossed the room slowly, then placed a hand on Rook's shoulder. Firm enough to anchor him. Light enough to pacify resistance.

"Cassandra is not unstable because of you. Or even because of Harrow. She was caught in the vacuum—between his grief and your silence. The system failed her. We failed her."

Rook looked away, face tight. "I should have done more."

A soft chime cut through the quiet—a system alert.

Viktor turned, sharp. The conference table dimmed automatically, and a nearby panel slid open. A courier entered, face expressionless beneath a standard-issue Elsinore Analytics visor, a sleek datapad cradled in his gloved hands.

"Urgent transmission, sir. Encrypted. Priority tagged from Harrow."

Viktor's brow creased, faint tension drawing lines around his cybernetic eye. "Harrow?"

He took the datapad, scanned his credentials, and watched as the cipher dissolved, revealing a clean block of text—short, sharp, elegant in its restraint.

To the High and Mighty,

You should know that I am back in your domain—alone, stripped of assets. I will request an audience tomorrow to explain this unexpected return. I hope for your forgiveness, though I suspect I will not receive it.

—H

Viktor stared at it, jaw tightening slightly. He turned the screen toward Rook.

"Read this."

Rook leaned forward, eyes narrowing as the message flickered in the soft blue glow. "He's back," he said. "Good! I'll be able to look him in the eye and say—*you did this.*"

There were no theatrics in his voice. Just hunger. Grief hardened into resolve.

Viktor leaned in slightly. His voice lowered to a whisper into ears twisted by sorrow. "You still can do something."

Rook blinked.

"You can have your revenge, Rook. Something more than a play on his guilt. Not a street brawl or a public spectacle. Something clean. Precise. I will give you the moment. And no one will question it."

Rook didn't answer immediately. He just nodded slowly, understanding the price of what he was choosing to do.

Viktor nodded, then moved toward the window. Elsinore's skyline reflected in the glass, data towers flashing like signal beacons. His reflection merged with the city—the CEO and his empire, indistinguishable.

"If Harrow has truly returned," he said, "I'll maneuver him into a position from which he cannot escape. No alarm. No scandal. Not even his mother will suspect." He turned, glass of liquor in hand. "It will be done cleanly, naturally, it'll pass through the system without a glitch."

Rook straightened. "What are you proposing?"

Viktor gave him a calculating look. "There's talk in the East. Since you left, your name has traveled—attached to reputation, honor. A fighter. A swordsman of precision and fire. A man called Lamond—he spoke of you like a legend."

Rook blinked. "That was a training exercise. Nothing serious."

Viktor raised his glass slightly. "Serious enough for Harrow to notice. He heard. He listened. He … resented."

Rook tilted his head, voice cautious. "You think he'll answer a challenge from me?"

"I know it," Viktor said, stepping closer. "He's reckless and proud. Proud men walk into traps when the bait assaults their ego."

Outside, lightning flickered across the sky dome. Viktor's tone dropped low, cold, and exact.

"Did you love your father?"

Rook's gaze snapped to his. "What?"

Viktor didn't blink. "Did you *love* him? Or are you a dutiful son, playing the part of a grieving victim?"

"What kind of question is that?"

Viktor's next words were slow, precise. "Time fades everything. Pain dulls. Even rage. Unless you act while the fire still burns, it goes out. And then all that's left is memory and regret."

Rook looked down at his hands. His voice was tight. "I'll cut his throat in the middle of the atrium if I have to."

Viktor smiled. "No need for theatrics. We'll arrange something cleaner. A sparring match. A demonstration. Friendly, unsuspicious."

Rook was already nodding. "And we fight with live blades."

"One strike," Viktor said. "That's all it will take. Harrow won't question it. He'll revel in the challenge. He won't question the blades."

Rook's mouth set in a grim line. "But if he does?"

Viktor turned back to the bar. "Then I'll provide a failsafe." He poured another drink and hoisted it high. "A ceremonial toast, perhaps. A gesture of reconciliation. A chalice laced with something … irreversible."

He passed the glass to Rook. The two men stood in the blue glow of the tower, city lights blinking beneath them like data points in a dying system.

"This time," Viktor said, "we end the line. We leave no trace."

Rook took the drink, raised it slightly. "For my father."

Viktor matched the gesture. "For the future. For *your* future."

Their glasses clinked.

Somewhere in the distance, thunder cracked the skyline apart.

Then—a door hissed open.

Corra stormed in, breath ragged, eyes wide. The careful layers of corporate grace had come apart, revealing the rawness underneath. Her makeup was smudged, and her posture a wreckage of urgency. Every step she took carried an unbearable weight.

"One disaster after another," she said, barely audible.

Rook rose halfway from his chair, the hair on his arms prickling at the tone in her voice. "What is it?" he said. "What now?"

Corra's gaze snapped to him, and for a moment she couldn't speak.

"Your sister," she said.

Rook froze. Time stopped. "What about Cassandra?"

Corra swallowed. "She's dead."

The room shattered.

Rook staggered backward a step. "No," he said, but the word barely had sound. "No. No—how?"

"She climbed onto the floating gardens," Corra said, her voice fraying at the edges. "Out over the water. She was barefoot, singing to herself. She ... somehow, she ... she's gone."

Rook gripped the edge of the console, knuckles white. "She drowned?"

Corra shook her head slowly. "We found a tox-injector."

The same kind that had served spies and assassins during the Substrate War. That soldiers smuggled into the trenches to claim a painless death before the divine firewall was written to forbid it.

"Somehow, she was able to use it on herself."

Rook pressed a shaking fist to his mouth. He let out a sound—somewhere between a sob and a growl—and fell to his knees. "Too much death," he said, voice shaking. "Too much death already in my life." His fingers tangled in his hair, breath shallow, rattling. "I won't even cry," he said. "I won't ..."

But the tears were already there, flooding his eyes, his voice, his hands.

He crumpled against the cold floor.

Corra turned away, her face ashen.

Behind them, Viktor stood motionless, his reflection faint in the glass. The face that stared back at him was unreadable, polished, silent.

CHAPTER 29

"All activities, both public and private, may be recorded for audit."

—Floor 99 Safety Reminder Plaque

The funeral was scheduled for 03:17.

No reason was given. None ever was. That was protocol—early hours reserved for damage control and death. Executives grieved when no one was watching. Or not at all.

The chapel was silent, but not still. It thrummed faintly with server heat and whispered drone chatter, a room designed for optics more than mourning. Floor-to-ceiling glass panels cast a wash of cityglow over meticulously arranged carbon steel pews. Every angle optimized for surveillance. Three drones perched in the rafters, humming quietly—streaming the service for internal compliance review, should anyone need to verify that grief had been observed.

At the center of the raised platform stood a coffin. No more than a seamless black box, unadorned except for the scan code affixed to the lid, already partially peeled at one corner. It bore no name, no mark to indicate the contents were human.

Cassandra.

Not granted preservation. Not approved for memory storage. No posthumous uplink authorization. Her digital presence already scrubbed to compliance minimums. Her profile flagged posthumously for emotional volatility, anomalous system behavior, and suspected data compromise. All folded neatly under Section 88.

Non-executive clearance: *revoked*.

There would be no wake. No commemorative slideshow. No memory wall.

Only those willing to decode blacklists would even know her name.

The priest—a thin man with a dour expression, dressed in Elsinore gray—stood stiffly behind the coffin, reading from a hollow tablet. His voice was solemn and lifeless.

The words were sanitized.

Pre-cleared phrases about loyalty. Contribution. Sacrifice in the name of continuity.

No one cried. It wasn't protocol.

And then—

Harrow arrived.

He emerged from a shadowed corner behind the tech booth, where the lights didn't quite reach. For a second, no one recognized him. Blood was still crusted at the hem of his coat. Rough stubble lined his jaw. Unfiltered fire in his eyes.

Someone gasped. A ripple moved across the pews. Heads turned.

Systems pinged.

He didn't flinch.

He moved forward—deliberate, unarmed, unchanged. He hadn't slept. It showed in the stiff angle of his gait, the way his shoulders twitched like old code.

Rook sat motionless. He didn't speak.

No one did.

Harrow climbed the steps to the platform. The priest faltered but didn't stop recording. The drones zoomed in.

Harrow just stood there, staring down at the small black box that now served as a grave.

He lowered himself to one knee—slow, stiff, as if he were remembering how to pray.

Then he placed his hand on the lid.

Flat palm. No tremor.

"I wasn't there," he said.

A silence engulfed the chapel—real, total. Even the drones dimmed their hum.

"I should have been. I should've seen. I should have caught her hand before she ... Before the silence."

He rose.

Turned.

His eyes swept the room—across sleek suits and expressionless faces and the polished rituals of pretend humanity.

"But you built this."

His voice fractured—low, then rising, as if something cracked inside the ceiling.

"You forged a world where love is weakness. Where memory is a policy file. Where a girl like her—brilliant, kind, terrified—was told to optimize her output while she bled internally."

He locked eyes with Viktor.

"You put her in that coffin."

Rook stood up.

Fast.

The scrape of metal on stone rang out as his chair clattered backward. In a blink, he was on the platform, boots grinding through the silence.

He grabbed Harrow by the coat collar, yanked him back a step with force that came from somewhere far deeper than muscle.

"You—" Rook choked the word like it tasted of ash. Then he drove his fist forward.

Harrow didn't dodge the punch. He staggered with it, absorbing the blow like he deserved it. Or maybe he just didn't care.

"You," Rook said again, louder now. Like the word itself could wound.

Then he lunged.

This time, Harrow moved. He dropped low, the second swing slicing past his head. Wind rushed over them both. The drones adjusted focus.

"She trusted you!" Rook shouted. "And you left!"

The third strike came wild. Grief was making Rook reckless, and that made him dangerous.

Harrow caught his wrist mid-swing—one smooth, practiced motion. His fingers locked, thumb against tendon. Not enough to break. Just enough to halt.

"You think I had a choice?" Harrow said, voice low, every syllable honed to precision. "You think they gave me one?"

Rook's breath shook. His whole body trembled under the weight of restrained fury. He yanked his arm back and shoved Harrow again, chest to chest now, nose to nose.

"You think this *fixes* anything?"

Harrow didn't answer right away. He glanced down—just briefly—at the black crate beside them.

"No," he said. "But maybe it will start something."

Then he turned.

He faced Viktor directly.

"Set the terms," Harrow said. "Set the arena."

His voice carried, unflinching.

He turned to the room—the seated executives, the quiet watchers behind mirrored visors, the drones still circling like vultures. He addressed them all.

"This isn't vengeance," he said. "Just an audit."

A pause.

"If the system won't listen to ghosts—" he glanced down at the coffin "—then it can answer to fire."

The air shifted. Not a sound, not a motion—but something fundamental tipped. As if gravity was pulling them toward inevitability.

Viktor smiled faintly. A tired, indulgent expression.

"So be it," he said.

Behind him, the priest stepped backward, eyes wide, hands still clutched around his tablet. He hadn't been trained for this.

Security hovered, ready for action—but no one moved. Not yet.

Harrow turned back. One last look at the coffin. One last moment.

He knelt—just slightly—and ran his fingers along the smooth black surface. The scan code tag crackled under his touch.

"God be with you, Cassandra," he whispered softly.

Then he stood. And walked away.

CHAPTER 30

"NO TRADITION, JUST EXECUTIONS"

—GRAFFITI IN THE ALLEY BEHIND ELSINORE ANALYTICS

Pax found Harrow a few hours later out in the Neon, where the city's veins collapsed into static.

The old observation deck sagged like a carcass, being swallowed by time. Glassless window frames gaped into smog. The ceiling—what remained of it—arched above in fractured steel ribs. Incandescence from below barely licked the walls. The hum of ancient servers had fallen silent. Some of those servers had once routed wartime comms during the Substrate War—back when the Neon was a staging ground instead of a graveyard. Now they stood hollow, stripped of function, like the veterans who were left breathing but never whole. Everything smelled of ozone, rust, and decay.

Harrow stood in silhouette near the edge, backlit by the sick red glow of a dying ad-feed two levels down. His coat was shrugged off one shoulder, collar cocked. Hands bare. No gloves, no active implants. Just skin. He didn't need armor anymore.

The floor was coated in ash-fine dust that curled under Pax's boots. No one had been here in years. Maybe not since Elsinore's first expansion, when this deck still had a function. Now it was a relic—like Harrow.

"You look like shit," Pax said in a low voice.

Harrow didn't turn. "Feel worse."

Pax stepped closer. The air buzzed faintly between them—residual static from ungrounded tech. He glanced at the exposed conduits running like veins through the walls. Dead wires. Forgotten signal paths. Like this place wanted to speak but was too far gone to remember how.

"You shouldn't be here."

"I'm not supposed to be anywhere."

Pax didn't argue. He just moved beside him, standing shoulder to shoulder at the cracked ledge. The glass was long gone—replaced by sharp, biting air. Below, the city pulsed in broken rhythm. Transit drones flared and vanished. Data-haulers skimmed over rooftops like beetles. A city pretending to be more than the rot it was built on.

"They tried to kill you?" Pax said.

"They tried to *erase* me," Harrow corrected, the edge in his voice honed by something old and personal. "There's a difference."

Pax didn't reply. His silence was a small act of respect. He knew that whatever was coming next had already started.

"What did you do?" he asked, breaking the silence.

Harrow exhaled slowly through his nose. Then turned his head, enough for Pax to see his profile.

"I rewrote the order. Gave myself executive override. Routed the kill command into a recursive loop. Logged a successful termination and let a virtual corpse rot."

A flicker passed over Pax's face. He didn't speak, but his eyes betrayed him. Unease mixed with awe. Hard to tell where one ended and the other began.

"Keir?" Pax asked quietly.

Harrow didn't look at him. "He made his choice." The words were flat, but not cold. "I didn't mean to enjoy it. But watching the machine eat itself? Chewing its own wires. There was poetry in that. Beautiful, in a way."

The silence that followed was dense, metallic, heavy with shared ghosts.

"And Viktor?" Pax pressed.

"Don't you think it's my duty to kill him?" Harrow's tone sharpened. "He killed my father. Made my mother a whore. Stole the position that was mine by right. Plotted against my life with tricks so cheap they'd shame a street hustler. Wouldn't killing him be justified—completely justified? And wouldn't I be damned if I let this cancer keep growing?"

Pax frowned, his arms folded tight. "He's going to find out what you did in Neo-Paris. How you escaped."

"He will. Soon." Harrow leaned his head back, let the steel beams swallow his silhouette. "But I've got a little time. And it only takes a second to kill a man. The trick is finding that second. I don't want him to slip away clean. His death has to be seen. It has to be undeniable.

"Still—I regret losing control with Rook. I see my cause mirrored in his. I should've honored that. I'll try to win him back. But his grief—barricaded and subdued by protocol—" Harrow's lip curled. "It lit a fuse in me I couldn't smother."

"You have a plan?" Pax asked.

"Not a plan." Harrow's voice lowered to a whisper, dangerous in its calm. "A path."

Pax nodded. "Where does it end?"

Harrow turned back toward the broken city. Neon flickered against smoke, windows twitching like faulty eyes. Somewhere below, reality looped and crashed and rebooted, glitching as it tried to process a lie told too many times.

"With an audit," he said.

A pause. Then, softer—almost reverent:

"With fire."

Footsteps behind them—measured, echoing like punctuation in a silent room.

Pax turned first.

Reynaldo.

His suit was perfect: midnight-black synth-weave, lapels sharp. Gloves matched. No dust clung to him. No errant thread, no misaligned hem. A man forged by protocols, never questioning the result.

His face didn't move. He might've been printed, not born.

"Harrow," he said.

"Reynaldo."

"There is to be a duel."

Harrow didn't react at first. Just blinked once.

"A duel?"

"An internal petition has been ratified," Reynaldo said, stepping forward with bureaucratic grace. "Elsinore honors traditions in matters of dispute. Trial by combat."

The War left too many grievances unresolved. So the Board repackaged dueling as catharsis—blood in place of audits, steel in place of policy. Cheaper than trials. Quicker than tribunals. A soldier's ritual turned corporate.

Harrow exhaled a breath that wasn't quite a laugh. "How medieval," he said. "How ... efficient."

"Rook has called for it," Reynaldo continued, smooth as ice. "He is eager to demonstrate his alignment with Elsinore's values."

"You mean loyalty."

Reynaldo tilted his head slightly. "Loyalty is such a soft word. This is about resolution."

"No," Harrow said, stepping forward, coat shifting like shadowfall. "This is about spectacle. You want theater. You want a sanctioned purge dressed as tradition."

Reynaldo didn't blink. "We want finality. The Board is ... fatigued."

Harrow studied him, eyes narrowed. "If I win, he loses the right to hide. No more ciphers. No more proxies. He stands exposed."

"And if you lose?" Reynaldo asked.

"Then he writes the story," Harrow said. "And I become a corrupted file in someone else's postmortem."

Reynaldo gave no answer. Didn't need to. The terms were coded into the system.

"Tell Viktor I accept," Harrow said. A pause. Then, darker: "Tell him the audit begins with blood."

Reynaldo turned on a pin-perfect axis and walked away. His footsteps never faltered, never echoed. As if the shadows were trained to swallow him on cue.

He vanished like a redacted line.

Harrow didn't move.

Neither did Pax.

The silence stretched, full of static and low humming machines.

"It's a trap," Pax said finally, his voice flat, like he was trying not to give the words weight.

"Of course it's a trap," Harrow replied. His jaw tightened, his eyes on the darkened consoles. "What else could it be?"

"Then don't accept Rook's challenge."

Harrow laughed once, sharp and humorless, the sound bouncing off steel walls. "No, I'm bound to it now. Doesn't matter if it's rigged or not." He rubbed at the stubble on his jaw, eyes gone distant. "But something is off. I can feel it in my bones. Foreboding."

"You should listen to your instincts," Pax said. He shifted his weight against the wall. "They've kept you alive this long."

"It doesn't matter." Harrow's tone was resigned. "Nobody knows when they'll die. There's no use dreading it. Death shows up when it wants, not when you're ready."

Pax studied him for a long moment. Then he stepped forward, until his boots scuffed the ash at Harrow's side. "Then if it comes, it comes for both of us. I don't care what trap they've set—I'm not leaving you to walk into it alone."

Harrow finally glanced at him. An unreadable expression flickered across his face. He didn't argue. He didn't thank him. But he didn't push him away.

Far below, the city groaned—metal or machine or memory. It was hard to tell these days. The streets twitched in neon pulses, like nerves misfiring with each dying breath.

The sound carried up through the observation deck, through the vents and beams. Both men held their breath. And when the silence returned, it held them together at the edge, shoulder to shoulder against the dark.

CHAPTER 31

"A clean death preserves capital."

—Finance Division: End-of-Life Liquidity Planning

The dueling chamber had once been a demonstration arena—a sleek, high-ceilinged space carved out of the top level of Elsinore's operations wing, where tech prototypes and combat algorithms were unveiled for shareholders with a taste for champagne and blood. During the Substrate War, this same floor hosted "nonlethal" field trials—kill-logic sandboxes where civilian investors watched battle-field algorithms pick winners in real time. The champagne was gone; the doctrine stayed.

Harrow stepped through the double doors, shoulders squared, boots echoing on the hard floor. Above him, hundreds of glass eyes watched—real-time feeds piped into private lounges, boardrooms, subterranean bunkers. The betting engines still used Substrate-era triage models: predict the loss, price the grief, monetize the outcome.

A match like this was profitable theater. The betting algorithms had been recalibrated to maximize event wagers.

The air thrummed with potential violence.

At the far end of the chamber stood Rook—coat shrugged off, collar open, posture ready. His left arm, the cybernetic one, hissed faintly as it adjusted. He had tied his hair back. The look in his eyes wasn't anger anymore. It was cold and measured.

This wasn't just a fight between grieving men.

This was a sanctioned deletion. Elimination of unprofitable variables.

Viktor sat in his observation deck, lit by the faint blue glow of augmented glass. He looked down at Harrow like he was a bug in a jar—worth studying, but ultimately disposable. Beside him, Corra sat frozen, fingers tight around the stem of a crystal goblet.

Pax stood near the chamber doors, flanked by security drones. He'd tried to talk Harrow out of it. But his words fell on deaf ears.

A sleek table slid into view in the middle of the floor, presenting two identical weapons: steel nanofilament swords, edge-charged, practically weightless. The AI overseeing the duel spoke in an emotionless voice that contrasted the tension in the air.

"Combat begins on mutual readiness. Blade selection is open. No ranged augmentation permitted. Vital signs will be monitored for lethal thresholds. Executive override available. No appeal process exists."

Harrow stepped forward, boots echoing against the steel floor. Two blades waited on the altar between them, humming faintly, light crawling along their edges. He stared at them but didn't move.

Not yet.

Rook joined him, the cold air fogging from his lungs. "This ends today," he said.

Harrow's eyes flicked upward to the observation deck, where shadows shifted behind glass. "That's what they're here to see," he murmured.

Rook hesitated. His hand hovered over the left blade, knuckles whitening. The weapon pulsed, alive, as if daring him to touch it.

Harrow smiled—a thin, dangerous cut of a smile. "Afraid it'll bite?"

Rook closed his fingers around the hilt. Energy roared to life, snapping in the air. He raised the blade in silent answer.

Only then did Harrow take the right.

The moment he touched it, a quiet thrill ran through his AuRORA. The sword recognized him. It synced. Temperature, grip calibration, combat style preferences. All accessible.

But he didn't need help from the system today.

He wanted the pain.

He wanted to feel the weight—to test its balance.

A slow silence fell. Every sound compressed—like the world was holding its breath. Viktor gave the nod. The AI confirmed the match parameters.

"*En garde. Prêts? Allez!*"

The swords rose.

The duel started with each man tuning himself to the space, sizing each other up, gauging the rhythm of the other's breathing. Two predators in a neon cage. Every movement could be a feint.

Every pause, a trap.

Then—

Steel flashed.

The chamber erupted into motion.

Rook advanced and lunged.

The attack was graceful—quick and silent. Harrow saw a flash and instinctively parried before his mind was conscious of movement. The swords clashed in a blur of light, the electric whine of nanofilament blades crackling through the dueling chamber.

It had always been that way. Rook had honed his skill through discipline and necessity. His form and style were perfected. His muscles had memorized every nuance. Harrow had excelled in his training. His talent was obvious, but he leaned on instinct over form. Rook's flawless control and Harrow's erratic instinctiveness made them equals in the chamber.

This is different, Harrow thought. *He's not performing. He's aiming to delete me.*

Another lunge—clean, controlled, aiming low.

Harrow ducked, twisted. Used the momentum to spin behind Rook. His own blade thrust. Not the killing blow, not yet. A warning. Rook parried. Stepped back, recovered.

They circled each other, scanning for vulnerabilities.

Above them, the audience held still. Even the AI monitoring the fight adjusted its parameters, registering the increased velocity.

"Combat intensity: elevated. Blood pressure spikes detected. Internal temperature rising. Syncing live feeds."

Corra gripped the arms of her chair. Viktor remained perfectly still.

Below, Harrow thrust again. Faster now, trying to break the rhythm.

He was good. But Rook—

He didn't flinch. Didn't blink.

Absorbed Harrow's attacks easily.

He's been waiting for this, Harrow realized. *He's been preparing.*

Rook's next lunge landed.

Not deeply. But it burned.

A thin line opened across Harrow's forearm—sharp, stinging. He hissed and drew back. It didn't feel like a normal cut.

An uncharacteristic flicker of doubt crossed his face.

Rook didn't press. He didn't need to.

He remained there, sword raised, letting Harrow feel it.

The poison hadn't kicked in yet. But Harrow had already lost something.

His balance.

His illusion of control.

Across the arena, Pax saw it too—his eyes narrowed as he stepped closer to the glass.

Corra said, "Something's wrong."

Viktor remained silent, savoring the moment.

He already knew.

Harrow's grip faltered.

Only for a second—but in that second, Rook lunged with his cybernetic arm.

The blade found flesh again. This time, the cut was deeper.

Harrow staggered back, his shoulder screaming with a sharp, foreign heat. A system warning pulsed across the corner of his neural HUD: *TOXIN DETECTED.*

He blinked. His vision blurred for half a heartbeat before sharpening into something too clear—every light too bright, every sound too loud. His body had begun the slow, irreversible process of unraveling from the inside.

Across the chamber, Viktor leaned forward in his seat, watching. Waiting.

"Again!" someone said from the gallery.

Harrow raised his blade. So did Rook. Neither of them moved.

"You…" Harrow's voice was low, rasping. "You laced the blade."

Rook didn't deny it.

He charged instead.

Their weapons met again. Harrow didn't hold back. The clash sparked violently. The dueling chamber rang with the electric shriek of friction. Harrow parried, turned, pivoted into a precise cut. His blade sliced across Rook's ribs.

Rook gasped.

His HUD flared red.

TOXIN ABSORPTION: 0.8ml. Fatal.

His breath stuttered. *What —?*

They locked eyes across the chamber. Realization dawned.

"You were supposed to fall first," Rook said. "A nick to slow you. A lunge to finish you. A guaranteed victory."

And then the lie they'd been performing—this "friendly" exhibition match—shattered.

Harrow dropped into a defensive stance, swaying. Sweat pooled beneath his collar. His skin felt wrong, his muscles locked in unfamiliar sequences. Whatever was inside him was rewriting the code.

He glanced at the stands.

Corra had risen from her seat, her face a shade too pale beneath the gold lighting—like the color had drained out faster than the room could compensate. She reached for her glass, fingers brushing the stem with a kind of absent grace, as if her body moved out of habit, not thought. She picked up the glass next to hers. The one prepared for Harrow if he prevailed.

Across the room, Viktor turned sharply. "No."

But her hand was already lifting.

Too late.

The wine touched her lips. A sip—just enough.

Harrow watched it happen in fragments. Saw her fingers linger on the glass afterward. The slight flinch in her jaw. The widening of her eyes, confused at first. Then, in hatred, as understanding solidified.

Her other hand went to her abdomen. A slow, involuntary gesture. She could feel something inside her failing.

Her augmentations blinked—red, then nothing.

"Harrow," she said.

He was already moving. Stumbling forward, off the dueling floor.

Toward the box. Toward the end.

Rook grabbed his arm.

Harrow lunged wildly. "You killed her!" he screamed.

"No," Rook said. "*He* did."

Behind the reinforced glass, Viktor stood motionless. As if he could stop the world by refusing to acknowledge its presence.

But the world was moving now, fast and bloody.

For Harrow, the world slowed—enough for him to savor the moment when the last remnants of doubt burned away.

Corra lay slumped in her chair, her fingers twitching against the floor, nanofibers in her dress dimming as the poison crawled through her veins. Her lips parted soundlessly. Her eyes found Harrow's, and something passed between them.

Regret. Apology. The terrible clarity that comes too late.

Viktor didn't move to help her. Didn't speak. He stood there, hands clasped behind his back. Waiting for the poison to finish its work.

Waiting for Harrow to fall.

"You poisoned her," Harrow said.

Rook, barely upright, shook his head. "He poisoned *everything*."

Harrow stood slowly. His blade hung at his side, humming low. His breath became ragged. His limbs were fire and pain. He could feel the poison dulling his nerves—but not fast enough.

He looked at Rook, whose blood trickled down his arm in thin streams. His eyes were glassy.

"You're not my enemy," Harrow said. "You were simply another weapon."

Rook gave a weak nod, eyes fluttering. "He used me. Like he used her. Like he used *all of us*."

Up above, the guards began to move—too slow.

Harrow moved quickly, propelled by rage.

He crossed the chamber like a crashing wave, blade still drawn, eyes locked onto Viktor. The CEO's voice finally returned—he raised a hand, barking something Harrow didn't hear.

Too late.

The duel was over.

The real war had begun.

Viktor staggered back as Harrow advanced, each step closing the distance between predator and prey.

"You think you've won something," Viktor said, his voice barely masking fear. "You've won nothing."

Harrow's blade dripped with Rook's blood—his own, too—and still, he held it steady. "No," he said. "Not yet. But they're watching."

The crowd had fallen silent. Executives, advisors, the press feeds wired into the chamber's perimeter—all waiting for Harrow's inevitable fall. To fail, to *finish*. Instead, he turned toward the central holo-table, blood smearing across the console as he activated the embedded interface.

Harrow's voice rang through the arena.

"You want to know what this was?" he said. "It wasn't a duel. It was an execution. Planned. Staged. By the man you call CEO."

Viktor lunged for the panel—too late.

A flood of data burst to life across the central display: surveillance logs. Audio. Viktor's own voice, recorded and sharpened into undeniable truth.

"If the blade doesn't kill him, the drink will."

"Make it look like sport."

"*No loose ends.*"

Gasps erupted. The press nodes zoomed in like vultures to the scent of exposed rot. In the viewing decks, silent murmurs passed between board members, legal aides, rival firms already calculating the fallout.

Viktor turned to the crowd, eyes wide. "Lies. Edited. Taken out of context—"

"Rook," Harrow said, turning back to the dying man. "Tell them."

Rook, pale and shaking, forced himself upright with what little strength he had left. His voice was thin, but it carried. "It's all true. I knew my blade was poisoned. I let it happen."

He looked at Harrow. "I wanted justice for my father. But I became Viktor's pawn."

Viktor took a step back.

Corra lay dead in the background.

And Viktor was out of people to hide behind.

"You poisoned my mother," Harrow said. "You murdered my father. You corrupted my entire world and called it management."

He raised the blade again.

Viktor could no longer hide his fear.

And the whole city watched.

Viktor stumbled backward, the truth rippling through the arena like an uncontained virus. Executives whispered behind cupped hands. Board members reached for their comms. Public sentiment flickered in real time across floating holo-screens—polls, live reactions, hashtags that burst into existence and then collapsed like dying stars.

Viktor looked around, searching for something—*anything*—to save him. But his power had been digital, atmospheric. And now it was hemorrhaging.

"No," he rasped. "Listen—let's *talk*—"

"Talk?" Harrow's voice was smoke and static. "Like when you ordered my execution. When you smiled at my mother over my father's corpse. When you fed this city a lie and called it mercy."

Viktor reached for a security drone, a trembling hand issuing an override.

Harrow pounced.

The poisoned sword flashed in the light—then halted. Viktor's augmented hands clamped down on the blade itself, servos shrieking as steel ground against steel. Sparks spat across his knuckles where the nanofilament edge bit deep, but he held it fast, shoving the weapon sideways.

The tip jolted toward Harrow's throat. He twisted, straining, as every muscle in his shoulders burned, Viktor bearing down with mechanical strength. For a heartbeat, the blade trembled an inch from his own skin, his reflection shivering in the poisoned steel.

Harrow's grip slipped. Viktor snarled, driving him back step by step. The sword began to turn against him. Desperation took over. Harrow slammed his boot against Viktor's knee, wrenched the blade free, and threw his weight forward. The poisoned edge punched through armor, flesh, and the wiring beneath.

Sparks burst from Viktor's chest as the implants overloaded.

Viktor gasped, his back arched, eyes wide with disbelief—how could his power betray him?

But Harrow wasn't done.

He grabbed the fallen ceremonial chalice from where Corra had dropped it and shoved it into Viktor's mouth.

"Drink," Harrow said, voice cracked and burning. "This is your kingdom now. Cold steel and bitter truth."

Viktor choked, thrashing. The liquid reacted violently with his AuRORA—biofeedback flashing red in his eyes as the poison pulsed through him like fire in a data line. His hands clawed at the air. Then dropped.

And the CEO of Elsinore fell, not with ceremony, not with honor—a hard, graceless *collapse* into static.

Harrow staggered backward, one hand pressed to his side. Blood seeped through the tear in his combat jacket, dark and warm, a spreading proof of mortality.

"It's done," he said.

CHAPTER 32

"Corruption ends when someone exposes it. Justice begins when someone listens."

—Voiceprint Fragment | Identity: Harrow Eisler [Deceased]

"Harrow," Pax called, rushing forward through the chaos.

Harrow turned.

"Stay back," he said. His voice was low. Barely audible above the sirens that now howled through the dueling chamber as Elsinore Analytics initiated a full lockdown protocol. "If you touch me, you'll absorb the toxin."

"You're a bloody mess," Pax said gently as he knelt beside him.

"I was always bleeding," Harrow said. "You just couldn't see it until now."

Rook lay nearby, his breathing ragged, his skin pale. His lips moved.

"Pax," he said. He held something up in his hand.

Pax took it. A small disc, frayed at the edges. He glanced at the communication console, suddenly understanding what Rook wanted him to do.

Rook turned to Harrow. "Harrow …" A cough, thick with fluid. "Exchange forgiveness with me …"

Harrow reached for him with a trembling hand. They clasped forearms—soldier to soldier, sinner to sinner.

"You are forgiven," Harrow said. "You weren't the architect. You were only another pawn."

Rook exhaled once and was still.

Around them, the chamber dimmed. The power grid flickered, as if the city's central nervous system had hiccupped. Viktor's body remained in its twisted sprawl within the arena, a jagged monument to the lie that built Elsinore.

Harrow looked up at Pax.

"I told you to stay back," Harrow said, voice slurring.

"You think I care about protocol now?"

Harrow laughed, short and broken. "Listen and record every-thing. The rot went all the way down. The story they told you—it wasn't what happened."

"I know," Pax said, tears brimming.

"You don't," Harrow said, eyes slipping shut. "But you will."

He slumped against Pax's chest.

The crowd remained silent.

The city held its breath.

The last son of Elsinore—ghost, heir, executioner—was gone. And with him, the era he was meant to inherit.

Pax cradled Harrow's body, feeling the warmth leech away. His fingers trembled against the fabric of his friend's jacket—slick with blood, scorched with filament burns.

Above them, the lights in the dueling chamber dimmed further. The once-vibrant neon arena—designed for spectacle, for corporate theater—was now a morgue. The arena's pulse had stopped. The city's heart had stuttered.

Behind the reinforced glass of the executive suite, figures moved—but none approached. They stayed behind their walls, behind their protocols, watching the fallout unfold from a safe distance. Cowards. Survivors.

Pax laid Harrow's body down gently. "Sleep now," he said. "You've earned it."

He stood.

The chamber's central holosystem was still flickering, the stream still live.

Pax walked into the center of the arena. Every step echoed. He reached for the interface port, connected his wrist device, and the system recognized him. Security alerts tried to deny his access—but he inserted the frayed disc into the slot and the lights flickered.

The live feed stabilized.

And suddenly, every screen in Elsinore lit up.

Boardrooms. Subway terminals. Luxury flats. Bunkers and slums. Every part of the city, high and low, flickered with the image of a single man standing in a hollowed-out battlefield, framed in ghostlight and blood.

He took a breath.

"My name is Pax," he said, voice steady despite the quake in his chest. "I was a friend of Harrow Eisler."

A pause.

"And I am the only one left to tell you his story."

Images lit the screens around him—snapshots of Harrow's life, the twisted web of betrayal, the hidden data streams, the murder of Silas Eisler. Footage. Logs. Audio fragments.

Everything that Cassandra had gathered.

"I know you're scared. You're angry. You want someone to blame. But you need the truth. Not the sanitized press release. The real story."

He looked up. Into the cameras. Into the eyes of a thousand strangers and sleeping algorithms.

"Elsinore is broken. And Harrow died trying to show you the cracks. Now it's up to each of you to build something better. The Substrate War didn't end—it calcified into this. They told you it was history, but it only changed uniforms. The same algorithms that rationed life in the trenches now ration it in boardrooms. Harrow fought to drag that truth into the open."

He turned off the feed. The chamber darkened, its silence final.

Pax looked down at his fallen friend. For a moment, his throat closed, but he forced the words out steadily: "You've given us a chance. And maybe that's all history ever is—chances. Still … little hope is better than none."

He straightened, squared his shoulders, and crossed the dueling floor. The elevator shuddered as it carried him down, down through the tower's bones. Each floor that dropped away felt like a weight sloughing from him.

The atrium was flooded with light. He did not hesitate. His steps quickened, purposeful, until he reached the glass doors. One breath, sharp with resolve—and he pushed them open.

Sound struck him like a wave. Protesters filled the square, their chant fierce, unbroken. A thousand voices pounding in rhythm, not of despair but of defiance.

Pax walked into them, and the current caught him. Faces turned, eyes lit, voices rose louder still. He was swallowed by the multitude— but not lost. For a moment, it felt like the end of the Substrate War had finally arrived—not with treaties or algorithms, but with people breaking its grip together.

Collectively, they surged forward.